Weekly Reader Children's Book Club presents

# Freedom for a Cheetah

# Freedom

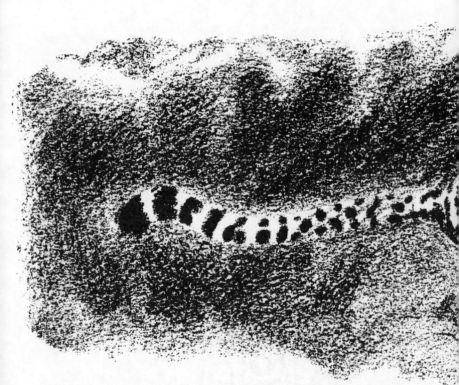

Lothrop, Lee & Shepard Co. / New York

# *for a Cheetah*
## *Arthur Catherall*
### illustrated by Shyam Varma

# Contents

# *chapter one*
# *Will the Cheetah Die?*

If anyone had warned the little group of men that Dum-dum, their cheetah, would be near to death by noon they would have laughed scornfully. In the warm yellow light of the early morning sun she was a picture of health. Standing three feet at the shoulder and measuring five feet from nose to tail tip, she was built for speed. She had the deep chest of a greyhound and long, powerful legs. Her coat of pale gold, liberally dotted with vivid black spots, made her a very beautiful creature.

No expense was spared to keep her in the best possible condition, for her owner was a wealthy

Indian merchant. He liked to bring business friends out to his country home to show them the cheetah at work. For him she hunted the speedy black buck, and many a guest returned home with a magnificent set of black buck horns as a souvenir of the weekend.

The distant purring of a powerful motor-car engine warned the men that their master and his guests were arriving, and last minute preparations began. Ram Chatterjee, Dum-dum's trainer, and his assistant, Shar Lal, a boy of sixteen, went over to the bullock cart on which Dum-dum crouched. Two scrawny village bullocks had dragged the cart here before dawn.

Unstrapping the soft cords that secured Dum-dum's legs to the metal rings on the cart top, Ram rattled the thin chain fastened to the cheetah's collar. She knew the signal, and leaped lightly down to the sun-baked ground. As yet she could see nothing, for a thin mask of soft leather covered her eyes.

In a cloud of yellow dust the big car, a newly imported Rolls-Royce, drove up, watched in awe by some of the helpers. At the beginning of the twentieth century automobiles were new, and only the very rich landowners and princes could afford them.

## Will the Cheetah Die?

At a signal from Ram Chatterjee the bullock cart began to trundle across the dusty plains, followed by the cheetah and her trainer. Shar Lal followed, holding the reins of two nervous ponies. Behind them, sitting in the open-topped Rolls-Royce, came Dum-dum's owner and his two guests. The trio carried powerful binoculars so they would miss none of the excitement.

The ungreased wheels of the bullock cart squealed agonizingly, but the small herd of antelope some four hundred yards away did little more than look up for a moment. They were accustomed to seeing the occasional bullock cart and knew the cart moved far too slowly to get near them.

This morning it was different, for behind the cart came Dum-dum. When the cart was within three hundred yards of the grazing herd the villager was told to stop. Ram Chatterjee quietly took the soft leather mask off Dum-dum's eyes and pointed the cheetah's head toward the herd.

For several seconds Dum-dum merely blinked. Then, when her eyes grew accustomed to the brilliant sunlight, she stiffened. She had seen the herd. Ram Chatterjee unclipped the chain from her neck and, with a whispered, "The big black buck, Dum-dum," urged the cheetah forward.

What followed next bore out the proud boasts of

11

her owner. Her belly almost to the ground, Dum-dum moved forward, slowly at first. She took advantage of whatever cover she could find, although there was little enough, for the summer sun had scorched the grass until it was withered and yellow.

A minute later a grazing hind looked up and caught sight of something moving. She must have made a sound, for the black buck also looked up. He did not see the cheetah, for Dum-dum had flattened herself to the ground, and her coloring made her almost invisible. The black buck advanced a yard or so, his head held high. His hinds gathered about him, waiting for him to decide whether they should run, or whether it was safe to stay and graze again.

A younger hind lowered her head and began to crop at the grass. Others followed her example, and finally even the big buck lowered his head. Yet he was suspicious, for within seconds he looked again, and this time he saw the cheetah moving.

With a leap that took him almost eight feet into the air, the black buck tried to get a better look at the possible danger. Dum-dum halted, but she was too late. She had been seen.

The moment the buck's hooves hit the ground again he gave the alarm. His hinds scattered with amazing speed. The buck, too, began to run.

Freedom for a Cheetah

The moment the hinds and the buck began to run, Ram Chatterjee, who had mounted one of the ponies, kicked his bare heels into its ribs and tore after Dum-dum.

The two guests sitting tense and expectant in the open-topped Rolls-Royce had never see a cheetah hunting. They jumped to their feet, binoculars clapped to their eyes, and watched with mounting excitement.

Fast though the black buck ran, the cheetah ran even faster. She seemed to go at twice his speed, covering the ground in unbelievable bounds until she drew level with him. An instant later the watchers saw a sudden explosion of dust as Dum-dum made her leap and brought the buck crashing to the ground.

What she had done would bring relief and joy to the people of a nearby village, for the herd of antelope had been stealing into their fields at night and eating seedlings that were due to be planted once the monsoon rains came to wet the parched ground. The death of the buck would keep the herd away and give hope to hungry people.

Ram Chatterjee brought the excited cheetah back to the rickety bullock cart. As he secured her on it, he did not see the rusted tip of a broken-off nail that was sticking out from the top of the cart. Leaning over to fasten the cord to Dum-dum's right forepaw, he drew his arm along the needle-sharp top and received an ugly gash.

He was trying to tie a piece of old rag around the wound when his employer saw what had happened. "It will heal soon, master," Ram assured him.

The businessman pointed to the gleaming Rolls-Royce. "We'll get you to the hospital as fast as we can," he said. "That injury should be disinfected and stitched. Otherwise, you might get blood poisoning. Come on. Shar Lal can do what is necessary for the cheetah."

"Yes, master," said Ram. He turned to Shar Lal. "You know what to do. Once you get Dum-dum back, take her out of the sun, give her all the water she wants, then feed her."

As the Rolls-Royce moved off, Shar Lal shouted at the villager whose cart was used for transporting Dum-dum to and from the hunts and, mounting one of the ponies, he led the way back.

Once they were at the house he stood and watched as the man propped the cart up and un-harnessed the bullocks. Then he hurried away to the servants' quarters for a meal, completely forgetting Ram Chatterjee's orders to see that the cheetah was taken into her stable at once and given adequate water.

Since Dum-dum did not run well on a full stomach, she never received food or drink before a hunt. By the time she got back to the stable yard she was already parched with thirst, and in the hours that followed, she suffered agonies.

Dum-dum tried to break free but failed. The sun beat down on her from a cloudless sky. She whined, but no one came to her aid. Finally she lay sprawled across the cart, her eyes closed, her pink tongue out.

By the time Ram Chatterjee got back from his visit to the doctor the cheetah was very near to death. At the sight of her his eyes widened. He lifted her head gently, then broke the silence with a thunderous, "Shar Lal! Shar Lal!"

His hands shook as he struggled to turn the limp body over so he could unfasten the cords on the cheetah's legs. He flinched as one bare arm came in contact with the hot top of the cart. It made him realize how much Dum-dum must have suffered.

Lifting the cheetah, he staggered with her into the comparative coolness of the stable and laid her gently on the straw. Clipping the wall chain to her collar, he got a big *chatti*, or earthenware pot, in which water was stored. Because it was made of porous clay the *chatti* was always wet on the outside, which kept the water as cool as if it had come from a deep well.

Dipping a rag into the water Ram squeezed a few drops into the cheetah's mouth. He could tell by her hot, dry skin that she was very close to heat stroke, and heat stroke meant death.

While he was struggling to get more water into the cheetah's mouth, Shar Lal appeared. His eyes filled with fright when he saw the cheetah lying so still. Ram ordered him to bring salt. Then he heaped several handfuls of it into the water and went on trying to give Dum-dum a drink. The salt in the water would help to cool the cheetah's blood and perhaps save her life.

An hour passed before Dum-dum recovered sufficiently to be able to lap at the water, and then the salt began to have its effect. Ram stroked her throat and massaged her legs and back. He knew all the tricks of looking after animals, and he *had* to save Dum-dum.

Shar Lal, who had stood watching in silence, finally plucked up courage to offer an excuse for not giving the cheetah water or putting her in the stable.

"Do not blame me for this, O Keeper of the Cheetah," he pleaded. "Before I could attend to the cheetah I was called away. I said that I had to attend to the needs of our animal, but you know what the house servants are like. They would not

17

listen to me and insisted that the master had ordered them to get me to do some work. I had to leave Dum-dum. I dared not refuse."

Ram Chatterjee did not reply for a moment. Squatting on his heels, he stroked the cheetah's neck as she lapped at the water. He felt sure Shar Lal was lying, yet there were servants in the house who might be stupid enough not to realize how valuable the cheetah was. Not even the wealthiest of the Indian princes could buy a cheetah just when they liked. A hunting cheetah had to be caught as a young animal and carefully trained for many months. To lose one of these graceful spotted hunters was a tragedy.

"Give me the name of him who called you away," Ram finally said, "and I will speak to our master about it. The man shall be punished."

Shar Lal gulped, swallowed several times, then muttered, "I have forgotten."

"That tells me you are a liar," Ram said coldly. "There are twenty servants in this house. If I tell our master just how near to death the cheetah has been he will question every one of them. Shall I do this? We could soon find out if you have lied to me."

Shar Lal was shaking in terror. He knew what would happen if the master of the house found out that he had neglected the cheetah. He would lose his job. Dropping to his knees, he said desperately, "O Keeper of the Cheetah, it was *my* fault. I was hungry, and after I had eaten I fell asleep . . . and forgot. Don't tell our master. I will take your punishment gladly."

"Gladly?" Ram growled. "We shall see." He went to a corner where some thin canes stood and, selecting half a dozen, swung them through the air until they made a singing noise. To Shar Lal he said, "I hate a thief and I hate a liar, but more than those I hate anyone who will hurt an animal, which cannot complain or hit back. Take off your shirt."

When he finally tossed the cane switch away he said grimly, "Next time you are tempted to ill-treat an animal remember this moment. I shall watch you."

Snuffling, and knuckling the tears from his eyes, Shar Lal hurried away. Ram spent the rest of the afternoon with the cheetah. He massaged her from top to toe, and when he was ready to go for his evening meal, he was satisfied that she had completely recovered from the horrors of the morning.

"It shall not happen to you again," he promised, running his right hand down her silky neck. "Since animals soon forget, you will scarcely remember your thirst by tomorrow's sunrise, but that lazy son of an idle father, Shar Lal, will remember his punishment for a long time to come. He will not let thee go without water again, not ever."

He made sure the cheetah's chain was securely clipped to her collar, and he also made sure the door was properly bolted. "Not that any thief would dare come in here," he murmured. "Dum-dum knows only me and Shar Lal. A thief would soon feel the weight of her paws or the sharpness of her teeth."

He stood at the door for a moment, considering whether to tell his master that the cheetah might not be really fit for the hunt planned for the next morning.

"If I do that," he finally decided, "I shall have to explain why she is not fit. I have punished Shar Lal enough. I would not like him to be discharged for his idleness. I shall say nothing and see what the morning brings."

He carefully bolted the big gates that shut off the stable yard from the world outside, then looked up at the darkening sky. There would be a moon.

He decided to take another look at Dum-dum before going to bed. A shaft of moonlight was shining through the iron-barred window as he peered through at her. She got his scent and sniffed eagerly, straining at her chain. In the moonlight her eyes were like green lamps.

"Sleep well, little hunter," Ram whispered.

Some time later, when even the lights in the big house were out, a figure slipped soundlessly over the wall of the stable yard. Keeping to the shadows, Shar Lal walked across to the stable where the cheetah was kept. He was limping, for his buttocks were stiff from the thrashing Ram Chatterjee had given him.

Sliding back the bolt, he opened the stable door and looked in. Dum-dum may have been sleeping before he arrived, but she was wide awake now. She stood staring at him, sniffing to get his scent.

"It is me. Shar Lal," he said gently, and when Dum-dum gave a little whine he walked into the stable. "Here, a little present for you," he added, and tossed a scrap of raw meat to her. It was a choice piece, stolen from the kitchen. He knew what the cheetah liked, and he grinned to himself as he saw how Dum-dum caught the scrap in mid-air. It was gone in a flash, and she licked her muzzle, purring with pleasure.

Still talking quietly to the cheetah, Shar Lal went over to her. He placed his hand on her head, slid it down to her collar, and unclipped the chain that held her to the wall. Then he drew her gently along to the open stable door.

Dum-dum went willingly enough. Most times when she was taken hunting it was in the quiet

21

dark that comes before the dawn, and she thought this was to be just another trip out after black buck.

The wooden village cart on which she was carried out to the hunt still stood there in the moonlight, but no warm smell of oxen came from it, nor was she asked to leap up onto the cart. Instead, Shar Lal took her to the yard gate. He slid back a bolt, opened the door, and led her through.

The land looked ghostly under the moon, but it was not the moonlight that made Dum-dum suddenly tense. The cool night air was bringing the smell of the nearby jungle to her, something she had forgotten in the two years she had been a captive hunter.

Usually when she passed through these gates she was on the cart, with the oxen plodding deliberately ahead. Men would be talking quietly, and occasionally a stick would whack down on the bony hindquarters of one of the animals drawing the cart. This night everything was different; there was something in the smells coming to her that made her whole body quiver with sudden excitement.

Lately she had been restless, and Ram Chatterjee had once or twice muttered, "Now that she's full grown we'll be having trouble. She'll want to find a mate." Dum-dum did not know what was the matter with her, but the vague odors drifting to her from the distant fringe of jungle were making her eyes shine with a brighter green in the moonlight. Yet she hesitated when Shar Lal suddenly gave her a push and said, "Go on, you're free. Get moving."

He gave her another push, then slipped back through the partly open door and hurriedly closed it, leaving only a chink through which he could watch what the cheetah did.

Of course Ram Chatterjee would know who had done this, Shar Lal thought, watching impatiently as Dum-dum stared out across the moonlit paddy fields. He'd know, but he wouldn't be able to prove anything, and so he'd lose his job. It didn't matter if Shar Lal lost his job as well. He was young and could find work elsewhere.

"Run!" Shar Lal ordered Dum-dum through the gate.

She looked around, puzzled. She had never been released like this and did not know what to do.

Had he dared, Shar Lal would have gone out to her and kicked her in the ribs, but he knew that would bring a lightning turn and a sweeping blow from a paw. He did not want that. "I'll get a stick," he muttered. "A poke in the ribs should make her move."

He hurried back to the stable, but when he returned with the stick it was not needed. There was no sign of the cheetah.

23

## *chapter two*
# *Hunting by Moonlight*

In the few minutes Dum-dum stood in the moonlight outside the yard gates a change came over her. She was filled with a new and strange delight. Her two years of captivity had been made up of long hours in the shady stable, and perhaps twenty times a year she had been sent dashing across the dusty plains in pursuit of black buck.

Smells coming to her in the stable had been mainly of mangy pariah dogs, which always made the fur on her neck bristle. The impudent crowing of cocks had been a sound in her ears most days. Mice crept in amongst her straw, and she killed many of them. The air had never been really clean.

The light breeze she was now sniffing with such enjoyment brought scents and sounds that thrilled her. Somewhere a jackal was howling, and when he stopped, a barking deer called. Both sounds were so far away that human ears could not have picked them up. Dum-dum heard them, and her eyes glowed. She did not know that when the barking deer called, it meant that a tiger or a leopard was on the prowl. There were many things she had never learned in those first few months when her mother was alive.

As she stood there, while the impatient Shar Lal urged her to "get going," a change came over her. Suddenly she knew what she wanted, and without a sound or a backward glance, she sprinted off in a direct line away from the big house. Her shapely paws threw up little puffs of dust, which looked like smoke in the moonlight.

The joy of her new freedom showed itself in her speed, for she began to bound in fifteen-foot leaps, slowing down only when her deep chest began to heave as her lungs cried out for air. To her right the dark line of trees that marked the beginning of the jungle began to thicken, until no moonlight showed in it at all.

Dum-dum was hungry, although that was not a

strange thing. She was always kept hungry. Ram
Chatterjee knew well enough that a well-fed
cheetah will not bother to hunt even the slowest
buck. Cheetahs do not kill for sport.

After running about three miles Dum-dum
stopped to rest. Now that she was out here she
needed food. She must look for black buck, and
when she caught one there would be no Ram
Chatterjee to snatch her away and chain her to the
cart again. This time she would eat.

Upwind of her a big sambar stag was resting.
Less than half an hour earlier he had had a lucky
escape from death. A tiger had sprung out at him,
leaping for the usual neck hold and hoping to
throw the sambar over and kill it in one quick
movement.

The sambar had caught a brief glimpse of the
dark shape as the tiger made his leap, and he had
managed to swerve. The tiger had been thrown off,
and was left yowling in pain and rage after being
catapulted into a thorn bush.

The stag had not got away uninjured; he had a
deep scratch on one shoulder. He was lying down,
trying to soothe the wound with his tongue, when
his scent carried downwind to where the cheetah
was resting. Rising, she sniffed the air. Monsoon
thunder was rumbling away in the hills to the north,

but there seemed to be little chance of the rains coming, for the moon shone brilliantly from a cloudless sky. If the animal she could scent began to run, she would see him easily.

Belly touching the dusty ground, Dum-dum began to stalk the sambar stag. As the scent grew stronger she began to tremble with eagerness. She was always like that just before a chase. It was as if she were charging up her muscles for the lightning-quick dash, which had never known defeat.

The scent grew so strong that Dum-dum could hold back no longer. She stood up and looked, and at once there was a grunt and a scuffle less than twenty yards ahead of her. The stag, getting no scent from her, had not realized he was being stalked until the cheetah rose.

With only a little eager whimper, Dum-dum rushed in. The sambar looked big and black, for he had his back to the moon. But he was no frightened black buck to turn and run. This stag was a veteran, and he behaved like one. As Dum-dum hurled herself at him the sambar swung his mighty horned head in a forward, downward, and up motion. Only a miracle saved the cheetah from being impaled on the daggerlike tines. Instead the stag scooped her out of the air and tossed her to

one side as if she had been no more than a bag of chaff.

A moment later the ground was drumming under the beat of the stag's hooves. He knew when to fight and when to run. Had he not run, Dum-dum would have been on his shoulders within seconds, for she had twisted like the cat she was as she fell through the air, and came down on all four feet.

Shaken and slightly bruised, she never hesitated. The drumming of hooves acted like a spur to her. She gave a little snarl and was after him at once.

The stag ran downwind, knowing that by doing that he could keep his attacker from getting his scent. Had the ground not been baked so hard he might have gotten away, for moonlight is tricky, but the drumbeat of his hooves kept Dum-dum hard after him. Within a minute she had cut down his sixty-yard lead to forty, and though he stretched his muscles to the limit, she still gained.

The sambar called on his last reserves for a burst of speed that he hoped would save his life. For almost two hundred yards he managed to keep thirty yards ahead of his pursuer; then his speed slackened a little. Desperate though he was, the sambar was too big to outrun Dum-dum. With the cheetah only ten yards from him and his heart almost bursting with the effort he was making, the sambar swerved to one side.

Dum-dum also swerved, but she lost a yard or so. She was only at her best over shorter distances, and now her lungs were beginning to protest. She cut down the distance and started to come up alongside her quarry, measuring the distance for a leap, when the stag swerved again. He turned right toward a line of stunted bushes that stood up above the landscape on a bank.

The bank ran along an irrigation river. During the rainy season it kept in check a tumbling, foaming torrent. In the dry season it carried a stream often no more than a yard wide. It was precious water nevertheless, and enabled the peasants to irrigate their parched fields. The banks of it were planted with shrubs to help keep the crumbling soil together.

The sambar stag knew the place well, for he often came here to drink during the driest of summers. Now he went up the bank with a rush and, for a moment, was outlined against the moon as he hesitated at the top. He made a magnificent picture, with his spiral horns pointing needle sharp to the blue-black sky. Then, with a bound, he was gone.

Dum-dum was only yards behind, and when she paused to steady herself on the bank top the stag was already scrambling up the other side. The man-made river was forty feet from bank to bank, but the moonlit stream coursing slowly down the center was little more than a yard wide. The stag had gone across in two mighty leaps, a magnificent effort for such a heavy animal. His first leap had taken him into the stream, and from there to the foot of the other bank.

After only the slightest hesitation while she gathered herself for the effort, Dum-dum made her leap. She aimed to alight just beyond the water and so avoid wetting herself. From there another jump would take her to the foot of the far bank and a third would take her to the top.

Straight off the bank top she went in a wonderful leap that made her seem to float through the air. As she came down her four paws bunched together to take the shock of landing. From that position she could leap again. She did not, of course, think how she did these things. They were instinctive.

This time, however, something went wrong. Dum-dum cleared the ribbon of water by a foot, alighting exactly where she wanted to, but then the very ground seemed to sink beneath her paws. On each side of the water was a stretch of mud with a thin sun-baked crust on top. Underneath it was wet and very soft. Dum-dum's weight as she hurtled down off the bank broke through the thin

31

crust, and her paws and legs sank into the slime below.

Not by chance had the sambar stag come this way. It was not luck that had enabled him to keep alive when others as big and as strong as he had been killed and eaten. He knew this man-made river; he knew about the mud. He had risked crossing it in a last desperate hope that his smaller enemy would not be able to leap as far as he could.

There was a sucking squelch as Dum-dum went into the mud and then, for several minutes, a splashing and a fear-stricken yowling as she fought for her life. Blind panic at this unexpected enemy only made her situation worse. As she struggled and thrashed about she only succeeded in churning the mud into an even softer slime. It got into her golden fur until she was covered from head to foot and looked far bigger than she was.

Exhaustion finally forced her to stop, and by that time she could only see from one eye. The other eye was covered with a blob of mud, and when she tried to paw it away she only made matters worse. Lying half on her side, she looked like a bulge in the mud.

For some minutes the only sound, apart from the throaty gurgle of the slow-running water, was Dum-dum's breathing. She had struggled until her lungs were crying out for air.

Her harsh gaspings brought an unexpected visitor. Looking like a ghost in the moonlight, a big owl swept over her, his eyes shining like yellow lamps. His down-covered wings made scarcely a whisper of sound, and Dum-dum cringed in new fear as he flew past her at a height of only a few feet.

She was startled even more a few moments later when the owl shattered the silence with a harsh *t'weet . . . t'weeet . . . t'weeeeeeet!* She heaved desperately in an attempt to get to a position where she could defend herself, but when the owl swooped it was not on her.

A few yards away a mouselike creature had been startled into making a movement by the owl's shrieking cry. Desperately it scampered across the mud, but before it could reach the safety of the water a taloned claw closed over it. Seconds later the owl was winging its way from Dum-dum, the first part of its evening meal dangling from one claw.

A dozen times in the long hours that followed Dum-dum tried without success to break free from the mud. In all that time the only living thing that came near her was the owl. The world seemed empty of life.

Then, an hour before sunrise, she heard a faint whimpering behind her. Struggling furiously, she half turned and saw a score of small animals lining the top of the bank.

The moon was waning, but it still gave sufficient light for her to see what they were: they were dogs. The sudden fear that had made her heart begin to thump immediately faded. She was not afraid of dogs. Those back at the stables had been terrified of her.

What she did not know was that these were not ordinary dogs. They were a pack of wild red dogs: animals that are hated and feared throughout the length and breadth of India. The only wild animal that did not fear them was the elephant. Elephants were too big for even the largest pack of wild dogs to pull down.

Once these dogs appeared in a district, nothing was safe. The wild boar, whose courage and fighting skill none could deny, would lead his *sounder,* or family, away when wild dogs appeared. He knew that not all his courage or fighting skill could defeat them. Even the tiger, ten times the weight of a wild dog, and capable of killing the largest sambar stag, left his kill if challenged by a pack of red dogs.

These animals were like a platoon of well-drilled soldiers. What is more, they seemed to have a code that said: hurt one of us and you hurt us all. If a dog was killed by a tiger, a leopard, or even the skulking hyena, the pack gave the killer no rest. Allowing time neither to feed nor to rest, they kept after the killer until sheer exhaustion made him an easy prey.

Dum-dum knew nothing of that, and she watched as the pack came quietly down the bank and onto the hard-baked mud. To them the trapped cheetah looked like an easy meal—not a big meal, but a snack for all of them. They had not had a good spell of hunting in the past days and were hungry.

Five or six of the older members of the pack began to walk up and down the edge of the soft mud, never taking their eye off the bedraggled cheetah. The rest of the pack sat and panted or scratched themselves for fleas. Dum-dum could do nothing but lie still in the mud, watching and waiting to see what would happen next.

She began to grow more and more uneasy as she watched the dogs. The calm, quiet way in which they seemed to examine the situation began to send little shivers of fear through her.

The leader of the pack walked slowly onto the softer mud, drawing back only when his forepaws began to break through the thin crust. When he seemed sure he could not approach that way he went upstream a dozen yards, then leaped easily across the soft mud and into the water.

Eyes glowing green in the moonlight, the rest of the pack watched and waited. They no longer yawned or searched for fleas. They were waiting to join the leader when he showed them how to reach the trapped cheetah.

Although the water was not very deep it was deep enough and the current was strong enough to carry the pack leader down toward Dum-dum. Then, as if some silent signal had passed between him and the others in the pack, an old dog and a young one, which seemed slightly bigger than the rest, trotted upstream and leaped across the soft mud into the water. They, too, allowed the current to carry them down toward the cheetah.

Dum-dum could do nothing but watch. She sensed a sudden excitement in the remaining dogs. The younger ones began to whimper and run backward and forward, obviously waiting for a signal.

Gathering herself for a last effort, Dum-dum struggled in the clinging mud until she had managed to turn around to face a possible attack. The first of the dogs was paddling easily only a few feet from her, keeping himself from being carried farther downstream until his two companions joined him.

When all three dogs were opposite her, Dum-dum snarled a warning, but it had no effect. The dogs were hungry, and she would be an easy prize.

At the moment Dum-dum was facing the threat of death at the teeth of the red dogs, her trainer,

Ram Chatterjee, was looking in horror at her empty stable. Wrapped in an old blanket against the chill of the hour before dawn, he had gone across to the stable to prepare the cheetah for the morning's hunt.

Within a minute he was calling for Shar Lal. Face contorted with rage, he held the broken collar in front of the youth and roared, "What have you done to me, you ungrateful dog? This collar showed no sign of breaking yesterday, and now look at it. The cheetah is gone. Who opened the stable door? Who opened the yard gate? I closed and bolted them! They were secure when I went to my bed. You have done this."

"No, master, no!" Shar Lal dropped to his knees, his hands clasped in a plea for mercy. "Why should I set the cheetah free? If you lose your position, will there be work for me? I shall lose my job as well. Some thief must have come in the night. It was not me."

By the light of the oil lamp the older man looked again at the frayed edges of Dum-dum's collar. He was certain Shar Lal had betrayed him. The cheetah would not allow anyone near her, save the two who cared for her—Ram Chatterjee and Shar Lal.

A few minutes later Ram asked a servant to take him to their master so that he could inform him there would be no hunting that morning. He knew what to expect, and when he returned to the stable yard, his face was strained and his eyes full of worry.

"I have managed to persuade our master to let us try to recapture the cheetah," he announced grimly. "If we fail to bring her back, we are both out of work. Go and put some food into a bag and join me here in half an hour."

"But we can't catch a cheetah." Shar Lal was aghast at the idea. "We would need wings to get near her. Not even with horses could we catch her."

"I'll tell you something," Ram Chatterjee said coldly. "Dum-dum is swift of foot, and she is young. I am not swift of foot, and I am growing old, but I have something she does not possess. In my younger days I was a *shikari*—a hunter. My father was a *shikari* before me, and he taught me well."

"You need a rifle to hunt a cheetah," Shar Lal said sulkily. "And will our master thank you if you bring him back a dead animal?"

"If you were not a stupid fool you would listen," Ram snapped. "Our cheetah is young. When I caught her she was no more than a kitten. She had learned little of that way of life."

"She catches the black buck easily enough," Shar Lal pointed out.

"Because *we* take her to them," Ram said quietly.
"We always take her within striking distance of
them. Unless I am an old fool, I think that within
three or four days she will be lean from hunger.
If we can get near her and rattle the tin from which
I always give her meat, I am sure she will be glad
to come back with us. And don't laugh," Ram said
angrily as Shar Lal sniggered in disbelief. "Go and
pack food for three or four days. You are going to
help me catch her, or I shall tell our master that I
am sure you set her free. Once he has got over
his first disappointment he will listen, for he is a
reasonable man. Do you come with me?"

Shar Lal nodded, then hurried away to persuade
the kitchen staff to give him enough food to last
for four days.

Half an hour later they walked out of the stable
yard, watched by several of the household servants.
Shar Lal carried a waterbag as well as his food.
Ram had a small bag of food and his old rifle. In
addition, he carried a leather collar, an eye hood,
and the long silvery chain to which the cheetah
was normally fastened in her stable.

"He's an old fool," one of the younger servants
jeered, as they watched Ram study the dust outside
the yard, searching for Dum-dum's footprints. "He
has as much chance of recapturing that cheetah as

I have of becoming a landowner. They say there is no fool like an old fool, and Ram Chatterjee proves it."

"He was stalking tigers and leopards before you were born," an older member of the household staff said quietly. "Why shouldn't he be able to stalk the cheetah? It wouldn't surprise me at all if they returned within a week, bringing the cheetah with them."

"I'd drop dead with surprise," was the scornful reply.

"In that case I'll start looking for someone to take your place on the kitchen staff," another of the servants said, chuckling. "I think Ram *will* catch the cheetah. I've never met anyone as clever with animals. If he says he'll bring the cheetah back —he will."

# chapter three
# The Wilderness Is Cruel

Held fast in the mud, Dum-dum was forced to watch while the leader of the wild dogs and his two companions floated down the narrow stream until they were all opposite where she was held prisoner.

Then the pack leader gave a whimpering signal —for wild dogs do not bark—to show that he was going to leap. The other dogs were ready to attack, too, one from the right, one from the left.

However, they made one mistake. They had not realized that the bottom of the stream was soft mud. It robbed them of half their spring. The leader fell short, and Dum-dum, somehow rearing a little in

41

the mud, brought down her right paw on the wild dog's head. The blow drove him face down in the mud.

The other dogs were also short in their leaps. Dum-dum managed to turn on the dog to her left. Her slashing bite left him with a tattered ear. The third dog scarcely rose out of the water. When he tried to spring, his hind paws sank in a hole, and his leap was a failure.

In a matter of seconds the whole situation changed. Instead of having an easy meal, the pack could only watch anxiously while their leader struggled for his life in the clinging mud. He was sprawled helplessly, his head held down by the cheetah's forepaws. His two helpers were also powerless to get at Dum-dum. The mud that had held her prisoner was now turning out to be a friend.

Finding new hope and strength, Dum-dum used the leader of the red dogs as a stepping stone. Pressing down on his head she managed to heave her body and her hind legs out of the slimy mud. She was not a pretty picture, for she was covered from head to foot—not one square inch of her golden hide was free from mud.

She did not get free easily. The mud sucked and squelched horribly as she finally pulled herself out of its clinging grip. The dog on whose head and shoulders her forepaws rested was also fighting for his life. With a last terrible effort he got his head out of the mud. His heave slithered Dum-dum forward and into the slow-flowing stream.

Like a little island of mud she floated on the surface, carried along by the current. For the moment she was too exhausted to do more than paddle to keep herself afloat. Behind her the leader of the wild dog pack had got his head into the air and was filling his lungs in great strangling sobs. He would live. But now he was as much a prisoner of the clinging mud as the cheetah had been.

Several of the younger dogs in the pack trotted slowly along the bank, keeping pace with the cheetah as she was carried along by the current, but whimpering calls from the rest of the pack made them turn back.

In the first light of the false dawn Dum-dum floated with the current, content for the time being to rest while the strength she had expended in getting free slowly began to return to her aching muscles. She had floated more than a mile with the sluggish stream by the time the real dawn came. As the sun tipped the far-off hills with gold, and light spread over the sun-scorched landscape, Dum-dum had a real chance to see where she was.

Rising five or six yards on each side of her was a bank with shrubs on top. The water was a yard wide, and between it and firmer ground was the mud—mud with a treacherously thin surface, which looked hard, but would not bear the weight of a cheetah.

The sun was well up when she saw a bridge. It was a rather precarious rope bridge, built by peasants so that they could cross from one side of the river to the other when the monsoon rains had filled it with rushing, swirling floods. There was another way to cross, but it could only be used during the dry season. The same peasants had laid a line of stepping stones from one bank to the other.

Dum-dum saw the bridge, but it was too high above her to be of use. Then she was swept against a large stepping stone, set in the very middle of the water. She bumped round it and was past before she realized that here might be a chance of life.

Desperately she began to swim, and because the current was so sluggish she got back to the stone. Painfully she heaved herself up on it and lay down. The stone felt warm and comforting. It was the most solid thing she had touched since taking that wild leap in pursuit of the sambar stag.

Forgetful of the red dog pack, Dum-dum closed her eyes and slept. Had the pack come downstream they could have torn her to shreds before she had properly wakened, for her sleep was deep and soothing, the sleep of a very tired animal.

The hot sun on her back woke her an hour and a half later. While she had been lying there the heat had baked the mud into her fur until, shake herself as she would, she could not get it off.

It was thirst that finally showed her how to get rid of the mud. After drinking she put first one forepaw in the water, then the other, and as the mud softened she licked and licked until the golden hair began to show.

Her bath took over an hour, for the mud was caked and had gone right down through the fur to the skin. Yet when she finally shook herself, every last speck of dirty mud had gone. From the top of her rounded ears to the last hair on her slinky tail, she gleamed, pale gold with black dots on her back and sides.

She bounded lightly from stepping stone to stepping stone until she reached the bank, where steps had been cut for the peasants. Not even looking at the steps, Dum-dum went up the six feet of banking in one graceful leap. The rest she had had and the long, patient washing had soothed her muscles, so that she felt as lithe and strong as ever.

Already she had forgotten the terrors of the night,

the mud, and the wild red dogs. Since animals forget the past and do not worry about the future, Dum-dum was now only concerned with getting food. She was hungry, really hungry. Had she been back at the big house, Ram Chatterjee would have brought her a basin of meat. She had grown accustomed to regular meals, a thing the wilderness never provides for the hunter.

From the top of the riverbank she looked around. To the north there was a dark green line, showing where the jungle began. To the south everything was parched yellow and almost completely flat. The crops had been gathered in months before, and the whole countryside was baked and waiting for the monsoon rains.

There was a promise of the rains farther north where the sky had a lead color. From that direction came a mutter and rumble of distant thunder. Dum-dum knew nothing of the rainy season. Her master never went hunting in the monsoon, so she was always kept safe, dry, and warm in the stable.

Blending with the color of the countryside, she wandered eastward until the light breeze brought the smell of antelope to her. Any other cheetah would have stopped and not moved again until it was sure where the smell came from, and had found the best way to get near enough to make a kill.

Dum-dum knew nothing about ordinary hunting. When Ram Chatterjee took the leather hood off her eyes she could be sure the big buck she was to chase would be within striking distance.

The antelope Dum-dum smelled were some six hundred yards away, and so keen was her hunger that she started to run immediately. She was going at full speed when a watchful hind saw her. She gave the alarm, and a buck leaped high into the air to get a better view of Dum-dum. Moments later the herd scattered.

The chase lasted less than half a mile, and there was no kill. The big buck had too great a start, and was still running strongly when Dum-dum slowed down. Over a distance of four or five hundred yards there are few animals to equal a cheetah in speed, but if a kill has not been made in that distance, most of them give up. They are short-distance runners.

Dum-dum watched the antelope race away until they were lost in the haze, then she turned north. Up there a line of trees showed where the jungle began. By now the sun was very hot, and she needed shade almost as much as she needed food.

As she hurried through the first fringe of the jungle a light breeze brought smells to her that made her eyes suddenly glow. She did not recognize

47

the scent of langur monkeys, but that of jungle fowl she did know. There had been hens and cocks living in the stable yard, and Dum-dum had eaten one cock.

The impudent bird had strutted into the stable one hot day when Ram Chatterjee had left the door open to allow air into the place. The cock had looked around. Then, raising himself as high as he could and puffing out his silly chest, he had started a boastful *cock-a-doodle-do*. It was the last boastful crowing he ever did. He made a tasty mouthful for Dum-dum, although the feathers had been a nuisance, making her cough and sneeze.

Now, as she walked through the first fringe of trees, she got the scent of jungle fowl, and quickened her pace. Even a mouthful of food would be better than nothing.

There were few sounds, save the never-ending drone and hum of insects, until a black bird, perched thirty feet above the ground, saw her and gave a piercing cry as it flew past her, scarcely a dozen feet away. Even when the bird had vanished she heard the cry repeated time and time again, loud and shrill.

It was a drongo, a bird not unlike a crow, and its call was one of the jungle's alarm cries. When the drongo called, it was a warning to all who cared to hear that a hunter was on the prowl.

Even if the drongo had not kept on with its shrill whistling warning, there were other sounds to give the alarm. At a time when shade is most needed, the trees of India shed their leaves. They lie thickly on the ground where, in the fierce heat of the sun, they quickly dry and become so brittle that when a foot is placed on one it crackles and breaks up.

Dum-dum knew almost nothing of hunting skills, and as she walked along sniffing the hot air, she took no heed of where she placed her paws. As a result there was a continual crackling of dead leaves underfoot to tell of her coming. She was too hungry to worry. She had the scent of jungle fowl in her nostrils, and the scent was growing stronger. Her eyes were gleaming, and her tail swayed almost jerkily from side to side, to tell of muscles beginning to tense for a leap.

Yet even she, with so little experience of the jungle, began to slow her pace as the scent grew stronger. Peering through the bushes at the edge of a small clearing she saw a smart little jungle cock and his family of ten hens. The cock was hardly a foot high, but he made a brilliant picture in his feathers of red, metallic green, and black. His hens were a very sober brown.

They were all busy, scratching among the litter of dead leaves for the countless thousands of ants that swarmed on the ground. Dum-dum's eyes were blazing with excitement as she sank belly to the ground, inching her feet into a position from which she could make a steel-muscled spring.

The birds were all within range, but two of them were close enough to be caught in a single leap. The cock, *tuk-tukking* to a favorite hen, had uncovered something special that he wanted her to eat.

Dum-dum's tail, which had been swinging gently from side to side as she got into position, ceased moving. It was the moment before she made her leap, and in that instant the gaudy little cock gave a single throaty *tuk!*

As Dum-dum leaped the air was filled with the wild flapping of wings. The sudden explosion of sound startled the cheetah, but even if she had not been startled, she would have caught nothing.

The little cock had heard her coming—the crackle of leaves under her paws had warned him. He had clucked a warning to his wives, and they were all ready, despite the fact that they had kept on scratching and pecking.

His bright eyes alert, the cock had seen the cheetah reach the bushes. Crouched low though she was, and partially hidden by brushwood, one thing gave her away: her tail. It had been visible, twitching from side to side. That little cock knew all the danger signs, and when the tail stopped twitching he gave his warning.

As a result the only thing Dum-dum got for her magnificent leap was a feather from the cock's tail. A wildly swept paw almost knocked the little bird out of the air, plucking out that single feather, which floated gently down to the ground.

Snarling in angry disappointment, Dum-dum glared up at a branch a dozen feet above her. The jungle fowl were perched there, busily shaking their ruffled feathers into place, and clucking softly. They seemed not the least bit upset. Dum-dum did not know that practically every four-footed hunter liked jungle fowl. Alarms like this one happened almost every day, and the birds were always on the alert.

They looked near enough to be caught, and after staring at them for a few moments Dum-dum made a mighty leap upward. She did not try to reach the branch, but aimed for the tree trunk. If she could dig her claws into the bark for an instant, another leap might get at least one of the birds before they could fly out of reach.

For a leopard or a tiger it would have been possible, for those animals have long, curved claws. Dum-dum's claws were short and blunted. The startled jungle fowl took flight even while her

claws were scraping madly at the bark of the tree
and failing to give her any grip at all. She began
to slide backward, then spun around with amazing
agility. A moment later, while the startled jungle
fowl were still flapping wildly to branches higher
up, she was back among the dead leaves.

Angrily she glared up at the branches, but the
last of the jungle fowl had just alighted safely alongside the cock. They were well out of reach, and
with another snarl Dum-dum strode away.

Success and failure teach the hunter, and the
next time she saw jungle fowl she would remember
how alert they were, and how quick to get off the
ground. She padded on through the trees, and there
was nothing to see, save the occasional brilliantly
colored butterfly. One fluttered so close that she
lifted a paw at it, but failed to knock it down.

The heat grew more oppressive and, finding a
shady spot, she lay down, closed her eyes, and
catnapped. At every sound she opened one eye.
Now and again there would be a burst of birdsong
from the massed and leafless branches, which spread
like a roof above her. Yet each time she looked up
there was nothing worthwhile to see.

Twenty minutes later she was brought to her
feet in startled amazement as the steady buzz of
insects and the intermittent twitter of birds were

drowned for a moment by a terrified screech. It was cut short as if whatever made the sound had been dragged into a room and the door shut, or a gag had been clapped across its mouth.

The fur around Dum-dum's neck and shoulders rose until it looked like an inch-thick collar. She stood with every muscle taut, ready to leap if danger threatened. For perhaps ten seconds after that short, sharp screech there was a shocked silence. Then came a roaring babel of sounds, a hullabaloo, which sent birds in the treetops soaring high in terror-stricken flight.

Her rounded ears turned in the direction of the sound, Dum-dum listened. To human ears it might have been the roaring of an angry mob. There was a mingling of screeches, screams, roars, and yells. Then came a crashing from the treetops and, looking up, she saw a number of langur monkeys swinging through the branches.

Dum-dum had a momentary glimpse of black faces surrounded by a silvery fringe of whiskers. Branches swayed down and creaked alarmingly as the monkeys swung with amazing precision through the air. They were all rushing in the direction of the strange hubbub, which still drowned almost every other sound.

Dum-dum began to hurry through the jungle in

the same direction. Anything that made a noise must be alive, and she was desperately in need of food.

This was the first time Dum-dum had heard a family of angry monkeys mobbing a tiger, for the langurs lived in the trees and rarely came down to the oven heat of the plains. Had she known what lay ahead Dum-dum would have turned and gone the other way, for there are few animals in the Indian jungle capable of facing a tiger and winning the battle. What was more, the tiger she was hurrying toward was in a very bad temper.

During the night the tiger had killed a big sambar stag and, after dragging the body to a clearing, had eaten a terrific meal. By the time he had devoured about forty pounds of meat the dawn had come and the rising sun was golden on the distant hills. Leaving his prize, the tiger stalked quietly off to look for water.

He knew all the places, and presently was drinking at a tiny pool, where a spring bubbled up from the base of a rock. He drank his fill, then carefully washed his face and his whiskers. By that time the jungle was alive with birdsong. It was a warning to the tiger of the danger to his prize from vultures.

Nothing was safe from these sky-borne scavengers unless it was well hidden. Quickly he retraced his steps to make sure the carcass of the sambar was not stripped to the bone by thieves from the sky or four-footed thieves from the jungle.

He was not in the best of tempers by the time he had gathered together some dead brushwood and dragged it over the sambar. The sun was growing hot, and the brushwood was like an oversized pincushion so that he had pricked himself more than once on the dagger-sharp thorns—some of them three inches long.

Finally he was satisfied that the sambar stag would be hidden from the keenest-eyed vulture. The brushwood was a yard high over the carcass, and around the edge he had scraped heaps of dead leaves. Nothing could get to it now without his knowing.

Yet there were two things he could not hide: the smell of the meat and the buzzing clouds of blow-flies already settling on the carcass.

He was ready to rest when a family of langur monkeys paused to look down at him. These silvery-whiskered animals hate tigers as much as they hate and fear leopards. Both animals can climb trees, and both have a taste for young monkeys.

The family watched in silence, but a young langur, looking for excitement, began to yell at the tiger. When his scolding and mocking brought no response, the youngster grew bolder. Swinging nearer the ground, he picked up a dead piece of branch and threw it at the tiger's head. His aim was excellent, for the piece of wood struck the tiger on the nose, a tender spot in any animal.

That was an indignity no tiger could ignore. His eyes blazed, and without any apparent effort he leaped upward. The great striped body semed to float in the air. The young langur began to shriek, and made a desperate leap for the safety of a higher branch.

His shriek was cut off midway as a powerful paw struck with sledgehammer force. Seconds later the langur was dead. It was so quick—like the crack of summer thunder—that it seemed impossible it could have happened. Yet a moment or so later the unlucky youngster whose daredevil teasing had invited disaster dropped limply in the litter of dead leaves. The tiger turned away as if what he had done was no more than the swatting of an irritating fly.

There followed a few moments of shocked silence, then the rest of the family came to noisy life. One and all began abusing the tiger, the older ones in deep booming roars, the younger ones screeching, and the females screaming. It was complete pandemonium.

The hubbub lasted several minutes, and stopped almost as abruptly as it had begun. A smaller family of langurs, the ones Dum-dum had seen hurrying through the treetops, arrived on the scene. They were anxious to know what they had missed. They were sure something interesting must have happened.

Their arrival seemed to make the larger group forget what the row was about, for monkeys have extremely short memories. A mother, with a baby clutching at her shoulder fur, gave a screech and bounded away. In a moment all the family were on the move, swinging through the trees like the high-class acrobats they were.

The young langur who was the cause of the uproar lay half hidden among the leaves at the foot of a sal tree, already forgotten. Yet even in that short time the body had been discovered by an ant, which scurried back to tell others of the find. In a day or so, unless some other larger creature found the body, the ants would have cleaned up everything, leaving only polished bones to tell of the tragedy.

Ignoring the row, the tiger walked slowly across the clearing and lay down behind a patch of lantana bushes. From there he could see his kill, and even hear, should any would-be thief arrive. He allowed his magnificent head to sink quietly onto his forepaws; his big yellow eyes closed, and before the last sounds of the fleeing langurs had died away, he was asleep.

Two minutes later Dum-dum arrived. She had been heading in this direction when the family of langurs went swinging away. As the hubbub died down she paused, disappointed. Her rounded ears flicked this way and that, trying to catch any sound, but the jungle had slipped back into its normal near silence. There were only the buzz and drone of insect life and the occasional shriek of a bird high up in the leafless treetops.

As she stood listening, however, Dum-dum's sensitive nose picked up the smell of meat. Her eyes lit up at the thought of food, and with new purpose in her stride she marched boldly along to the clearing.

Any ordinary jungle animal, no matter how hungry, would have paused at the edge of the clearing where the dead sambar stag lay. It would have kept out of sight while eyes, ears, and nostrils tried to discover if there was any danger about. It would have known too well that the jungle does not usually provide free meat meals for anyone.

Dum-dum had never known fear or the need for caution. From the age of three months she had been fed by Ram Chatterjee. Even hunting antelope had not been for food, since she was never allowed to eat her kill. All she knew now was that she was hungry, and that somewhere in the tangle of brushwood there was meat. With no thought of possible danger she stepped boldly out into the open.

Had the langur monkeys been there to see this madness they would have stared in silent amazement. This kind of impudence had brought quick death to their own foolish youngster. The tiger is the lord of his own patch of jungle, and other hunters are wise to keep out of his way. For an animal like a cheetah to stalk boldly out with the intention of stealing the tiger's kill is to bring a swift penalty.

Unaware of the risks she was taking, Dum-dum walked around the pile of brushwood to see what was the easiest way to get at the dead stag. After a moment she took the end of a thorny branch in her teeth and began to tug, trying to pull it away and make an opening through which she could get to the meat.

She never troubled to look around, so did not see the silent movement of a large striped body hidden behind the lantana bushes not ten yards away. The first crackle of twigs had penetrated the sleeping tiger's consciousness. He was drowsy after his heavy meal, but he opened one eye.

The eyelid was drooping again when Dum-dum

made an extra effort to drag the stubborn branch away. Again there was a crackle, and at that the tiger's eyes opened wide. For a moment he stared through the screen of bushes as if he could not believe what he saw. A yellow, black-spotted animal no bigger than a hyena was trying to get to his meat!

Silently he rose, silently he stepped from behind the bushes. A moment later he was bounding across the clearing. He was a terrifying figure of deep orange and black stripes, his eyes flaming with rage at the impudence of this would-be thief.

# chapter four
# A Fountain in the Jungle

It may have been some sixth sense that warned Dum-dum. Maybe her ears picked up the soft thump of feet on the hard ground. Whatever it was, she suddenly gave a screech and leaped to one side. The move saved her life. Even as she was leaping away the tiger was in midair.

His forepaws were stretched wide, claws extended. His face was a mask of fury, the eyes lit with rage. As Dum-dum leaped away the tiger landed on the spot where she had been, and his right paw came down with crushing force on the branch she had been dragging.

A *Fountain in the Jungle*

Then he shattered the stillness with a yowl of rage that made the fur around Dum-dum's neck stand up, every hair quivering. She had never heard anything like it before. There was blood-chilling fury and pain in the sound, for the paw that had smashed down with such force where the cheetah had been a moment earlier had struck a thorn. Dried by the sun until it was hard and brittle, the thorn was like a three-inch-long dagger pointing upward. The descending paw had come down on it like a hammer, driving the thorn deep into the pad, where it broke off. To the tiger it was like the thrust of a red-hot needle.

Blaming the cheetah for this sudden agony, the tiger turned and leaped a second time, and missed a second time. Dum-dum had never seen a tiger before, so when she leaped away from the tangle of brushwood, she had turned, ready to strike at whatever this enemy was. One glance at the massive bulk of the tiger had been enough for her. Her bound away from the tiger's second leap was the beginning of a terrified rush for safety.

She did not know that because of the thorn in his foot the tiger would not run for weeks. But she did know that she was no match for this great striped brute, so she ran with all the speed she could muster.

In her panic she blundered into a bush, and screeched with pain as several thorns went into her shoulders, one even into the top of her head. Yet she dared not stop. She knew she had escaped death by inches. Only when her great lungs were screaming for air did she finally fling herself down in a patch of long-dead grass.

Lying there panting she strained to catch any sound that would tell her the tiger was drawing near. Only when she realized the jungle was still quiet did some of her confidence return, and she began to think about getting rid of the thorns.

Her long rough tongue coaxed out all but the thorn in the top of her head. This one she finally broke off as she stroked her right paw over it. There was a quarter of an inch of it left, and it would have to stay there until it worked its way out unaided.

When she finally got to her feet again it was almost noon, and the heat was at its greatest. Even the birds were silent. The only feathered creatures flying were the vultures, tiny specks in the pale blue of the sky. They patrolled until it was too dark to see what was happening in the world below. For them there was no food until something died on the plain or in some jungle clearing.

Dum-dum was still hungry, but now there was a worse craving. She was thirsty. The long run had increased her need for water, but she had no idea where she could get a drink.

Unhappily she started to walk along, continually sniffing, continually looking, yet neither seeing nor scenting anything that would help her. Her tail was hanging low and her head was drooping when she finally stopped at a sound that gave her hope.

The jungle was beginning to thin out a little. Without realizing it, she had turned south to where the great plain began. Head lifted at the sound of falling water, she tried to locate it. In that hot, breathless jungle, the tinkle of water was the sweetest music any thirsty creature could hope to hear.

Ears cocked, she knew she had not been mistaken. Somewhere ahead, water was falling. It seemed to be within a patch of thicker jungle, and she hurried toward it. Inexperienced in jungle ways, she did not notice that a thinly marked track led into the trees. She was not the first animal to hear that water and to go in search of it.

Her meeting with the tiger had made her cautious. At the smell of food she had gone blindly into trouble, and had escaped the tiger by the merest chance. It was a lesson she would not forget. Now she listened and, with head uplifted, tested the hot air, but there was no sound or scent of other animals.

Cautiously she followed the trail through bushes, then into taller, older trees. Suddenly she stopped, her lips wrinkling back in a soundless snarl. Through the trees she had caught sight of a stone wall. It sent a shiver of fear through her, conjuring up a memory of the stable yard and of the building where she had been cooped up for so long. Despite her hunger and thirst, she did not want to return to captivity.

She sniffed and sniffed, but got no human scent, only the damp smell of water to spur her on, and thirst overcame her fears. After a momentary hesitation she moved forward again, the trees growing thicker with every pace until she was standing at the stonework itself.

Dum-dum did not know that she was standing at what had been the main door of a once magnificent palace. The stonework was crumbling now, although it still showed signs of beautiful carvings, a reminder that centuries earlier Moslem invaders had swarmed across this part of India.

They had conquered wherever they went, slaying and burning until no one dared resist them. When the fighting ended a palace was built for the man who was to be lord of this part of the land.

Slaves had hacked out a clearing in the jungle. Others had come to build the walls and lay over

them a roof. There had been high rooms for the sake of coolness, and long, narrow windows to let in air while keeping out the rays of the sun. There had been numerous servants, to swing fans, to fetch and carry for the conquerors.

After many years the power of the conquerors had ended, and the palace was left without ruler or servant. Then the beautiful gardens had become overgrown, and the jungle had crept nearer and nearer until finally it hid the ruined building. Roofs fell in, walls crumbled and cracked, and the palace became a refuge for wild animals.

The animals did not stay long. They usually came when the hot sun had dried up the rivers and the drinking pools, for the Moslems had left behind a gift of great value. It was a gift that neither the long years nor the power of the jungle could affect.

Moslem workmen had laid a pipe in the ground to bring water from the hills to the palace. That pipe remained undamaged, and in the main room a fountain played. The water still splashed down into a big deep basin, which had once gleamed with the whiteness of marble.

It was the sound of this fountain that Dum-dum had heard. The water gushed up to a height of three feet before turning over to splash into the basin. The basin was no longer gleaming white, for with the passing years a layer of green moss had covered it. Where the water overflowed and ran to an outlet in the wall there was another inch-thick layer of moss that looked like a deep-green velvet carpet.

Dum-dum was not interested in the colorful beauty. Much more important to her was the feel of the wet moss on her hot paws and the fine spray of cool water falling on her face. Dipping her whiskered muzzle into the big bowl she began to drink. The water was cool, and she lapped until she had drunk just as much as she could hold.

She was licking droplets of water from her whiskers when she heard another sound: a squeak, so faint above the splash of water that she could not be sure whether she had really heard it or not. Her rounded ears were the only things that moved. Like a beautiful statue she stood and listened.

When it seemed as if her ears had deceived her and she was beginning to relax, Dum-dum heard the sound again. Her ears flicked in the direction of some stones that had fallen into the chamber when the roof collapsed. The squeak had come from that direction. Very slowly Dum-dum turned her head and fixed her gaze on the spot, her eyes un-winking.

There was another silence, then from behind the

stones came a creature about the size of a half-grown cat. It was a bandicoot rat, and plump enough to take the edge off even a cheetah's hunger. Her eyes gleamed, but she made no move. The rat was near enough to its hole in the wall to get away if alarmed.

Squatting on its haunches, the bandicoot began to wash itself. It licked its handlike paws, then cleaned behind its ears with an almost human action. Dum-dum began to quiver with impatience, for the fountain was between her and the bandicoot. She would have to leap through the jet of water, and she knew that might make her miss her aim. Yet hunger had driven her to the point where she would have taken a chance when two more bandicoots appeared.

In the following five minutes Dum-dum learned one of the harder lessons of the hunter—the need for patience and the need to keep perfectly still. More and more bandicoots came from unseen holes. Some washed, others played, some just sat and did nothing; yet all kept on the opposite side of the fountain.

Dum-dum was beginning to despair. If she did leap she must make sure of a kill, or perhaps lose any further chance. If she frightened the bandicoots they might not come out again for hours and hours.

She was on the point of leaping and risking everything when one bandicoot hopped onto the edge of the basin and began to drink. It was the moment Dum-dum had waited for. A lightning-quick leap, and she had made her first kill since getting her freedom. The bandicoot died without a sound, without pain, and without knowing what had killed it. There were a few frightened squeaks, from the others, and when Dum-dum looked up the room was empty again. For a moment she was tempted to take her kill outside, but remembering the heat, she turned to a dark corner of the room.

When she went to the fountain to wash after her meal she was still hungry. The bandicoots might come out again when all was quiet. She settled down quietly in a corner, hoping for another tidbit.

Twenty minutes went by before she heard another faint squeak. Another minute passed and then a bandicoot came out. Like the first one, it sat on its haunches and washed itself. This bandicoot was a scout, and was here to discover if there was any danger. It was near enough to its hole to get to safety if even the slightest movement suggested that an enemy was in the place. The bandicoots lived dangerously and, like the jungle fowl, were always on the alert.

The bandicoots had been here for many years,

71

having discovered that there was seldom a shortage of food. Many animals came to the fountain to drink, and among them were tigers and leopards. When a thirsty deer came to drink and was killed by one of these lurking hunters, the tiger or leopard would eat its fill and then go away. The bandicoots got the leftovers. Ants cleaned up what the bandicoots left.

After finishing its toilet the watchdog bandicoot must have given some signal, for others began to come out. As before, they washed, played, and squabbled until, just as Dum-dum was getting ready to rise to make a second kill, the whole family of bandicoots suddenly froze, as if every one had been paralyzed.

They could not have stopped more abruptly if they had been toys worked by electricity and someone had switched off the current. Rats washing their ears stopped with paws upraised. Rats playfully fighting stopped in the middle of striking a blow.

Dum-dum half rose, and although for the moment she could see nothing, there was a prickling about her neck, and the fur rose. She sensed some danger—something she did not understand.

Seconds later she saw something moving on the far side of the room. Something long and thin had come along the passage leading to the jungle outside. That the bandicoots had seen the thing before was obvious. Their fear of it had left them unable to move. As a stoat is said to be able to hypnotize a rabbit so that it remains motionless, waiting to be killed, so the bandicoots remained as if turned to stone.

Dum-dum had never seen a snake, and she stared at this one in wonder. It was gray in color and some six feet in length. It had a small pointed head and lidless eyes. From its slit mouth a forked tongue darted in and out.

To Dum-dum the intruder looked harmless, yet she was uneasy. She had been preparing to leap, for she was still hungry, but the sight of the snake made her relax her taut muscles. Some instinct, passed down from generation to generation, warned her that this long wormlike thing was a killer, and far more dangerous than it seemed.

When the snake ceased gliding across the floor the only sound above the splash of water came from outside, where there was a growing mutter of thunder. The monsoon storms, which had been threatening in the hills for a week, had now arrived overhead. For the past ten minutes there had been an almost ceaseless rumbling as the black clouds thickened.

In that long-forgotten room in the heart of the jungle the rumbling of the thunder and the occasional flashes of lightning went unnoticed. All eyes were on the newcomer, which seemed to know that until it had struck its victim none of the bandicoots would have the strength to move.

Without a sign of hurry it began to glide among the bandicoots until finally it stopped before a plump youngster. Dum-dum watched, her eyes fixed. She saw the first two feet of the snake's slim body lift off the ground. Then loose skin at the back of the head began to swell out and at the same time it started to hiss.

On that loose skin, which swelled until it resembled a half-inflated balloon, was a mark that looked like a pair of old-fashioned spectacles. It was the mark of the cobra, one of the most deadly of India's poisonous snakes.

The head began to sway from side to side. It was a dance of death, for when the swaying stopped the narrow head would lunge forward. The snake would bite, and where the grooved eyeteeth punctured the skin a drop of poison would be forced into the wound. Speedily the victim would become paralyzed, and death would follow very soon.

The swaying head slowed its movements, but as it stopped the room was lit up by a vivid blue-white

flash from the world outside. Lightning had riven the dark monsoon clouds and, in less time than an eyelid can blink, had connected sky and earth. The flash lit up the countryside for many miles around.

The lightning was overhead, for along with the flash came a roar of thunder like the explosion of a mighty bomb. As the ground shook and the walls rocked there came another crash. The lightning had struck a giant sal tree, splitting it from top to bottom. The shattered tree fell against the crumbling wall of the inner room, and the impact knocked a dozen pieces of masonry off the top and into the room itself.

There was a rumble and a thudding as the stones fell onto the stone floor and rolled off one another. For the bandicoot chosen to die it was the luckiest moment ever. The flash and the following thunder made the cobra hesitate, and the narrow head half turned.

The uproar broke the spell that had held all the bandicoots petrified. There was a chorus of squeaks, and among the panic-stricken runners was the one chosen to die. It had gone into its hole before the cobra could turn and strike.

Dum-dum had been as startled as any of the others in the room, but she recovered as a bandicoot came racing toward her. In his panic he had forgotten where his hole was. She killed him as quickly and cleanly as she had killed the first bandi-coot. Her eyes blazing a challenge, Dum-dum placed a paw on the dead bandicoot and dared the cobra to come nearer.

Having missed its intended prey, and with the cheetah the only other living thing in sight, the cobra slithered around the side of the fountain bowl, hissing angrily. Not having eaten for ten days—the usual time between meals—the cobra was hungry. It had seen Dum-dum kill the bandicoot and meant to rob her of it.

Drawing her prize under her, Dum-dum snarled another warning and moved forward half a pace. She was ready to fight, yet there was something about the snake that sent a little shiver of fear through her. The cobra slithered nearer. It was hungry, and few animals dared defy it. At Dum-dum's snarl it rose again and began a fresh dance of death. The hooded head swayed from side to side while the quivering tongue darted in and out, in and out. Dum-dum snarled, but it was a halfhearted snarl. She was coming under the same hypnotic spell that had made the bandicoots stand helpless while the cobra chose its victim.

The swaying grew less, and suddenly Dum-dum whimpered as something struck her tender black nose.

## chapter five
# Ten Thousand Enemies

The cobra had steadied itself for a quick lunge forward and a bite with its incurving teeth, but the lunge was never made. As Dum-dum stiffened and whimpered at the pain on her nose, the cobra turned and fled. It raced across the floor as fast as it could, while a buzzing cloud of bees hovered over it and settled on it.

The lightning that had ripped the sal tree from top to bottom had also started a fire in the dry undergrowth near the tree's roots. When the shattered half of the tree fell against the wall of the old palace and knocked stonework off the top, the falling stones had dislodged three straw-colored globes clinging high on the wall. They were the nests of wild bees, and when they hit the ground they were smashed open. Out of them poured a host of furious insects, looking for the enemy that had destroyed their home.

Dum-dum's halfhearted snarl when she faced the cobra had attracted the attention of the bees, and the pain that had made her whimper had been a sting on her nose.

The cloud of insects settled on cobra and cheetah alike, stinging furiously. Dum-dum yelped and, brushing a bee off her ear, leaped forward wildly. Surrounded by the angry, buzzing horde, the cheetah would have been stung to death if that first wild leap had not landed her in the one place where she would be safe. Her eyes shut against the deadly attackers, she dropped with a tremendous splash into the big stone basin where the fountain splashed and gurgled.

Even in those few seconds Dum-dum had received a dozen stings, and she was glad to lie in the cool water for relief. There was another stabbing pain in one ear as a bee that had not been washed off drove in its sting. It forced her to duck under the water. While she was out of reach, thousands of bees buzzed angrily just above the surface.

The cobra got halfway down the passage to the jungle beyond, then stopped. It could not endure the stings. Hidden under a swarming mass of bees, it rolled and writhed, squashing hundreds of its attackers. But it could not win. For years it had come into the ruined palace every time it needed a meal. It had been an easy life. A quick bite from its poisoned fangs, an equally quick wrapping of its coils about a terrified bandicoot, holding it until the poison did its work, and then a feast. The cobra, who had killed so many with poison, now died in the same way as the bees stung and stung.

Outside there was a hollow roaring as flames from the fire started by the flash of lightning spread rapidly in the dead, and very dry, undergrowth. The windows of the palace, shrouded by spiders' webs, began to glow pink as the flames took fiercer hold.

The air was filled with a snapping and a crackling, for the ground was thick with the dead leaves of many years. Everything was so tinder dry that even a spark would have started a fire, let alone a flash of lightning. Long after the fire had burned itself out there would be a black scar in this part of the jungle.

Lying completely submerged in the water, Dum-dum only dared lift her nostrils ino the air when her lungs felt as if they were bursting. Even so, she was stung, and drew herself under again. Again she lifted her nostrils for air and again she was stung. The third time there was only a distant angry buzz. With the sudden disappearance of the cheetah, out of their reach beneath the water, the bees concentrated on the cobra.

When it was dead they were faced with a new enemy against which not all their stings could avail. The fire outside the old palace walls was growing in fury and beginning to fill the air with smoke and fumes.

Even the bandicoots were being forced from their holes by the growing heat at ground level. They rushed out and fled for the open, and were pursued by new swarms of bees, forced by the heat and smoke from the undamaged nests.

Within ten minutes of the time the lightning struck the tree there was not a bandicoot in the place—or a live bee. The cobra lay in a coiled heap in the passage, and nearby were several dead bandicoots, which had also felt the fury of the bees' stings.

The fountain still sprayed the air, but now the walls of the room were lit by the fire, which had begun to burn the creepers growing up them. Smoke was crawling like red fog over the window ledges and down to the floor.

Dum-dum kept lifting her nose above the water to breathe, but she began to splutter a little as the smoke grew thicker and thicker in the air. The fire was now creeping along the tree branches that spread across the roofless room. Before long the ruins would be surrounded by a sea of flame.

Coughing and choking in the smoke-filled air, Dum-dum heaved herself out of the water. Better to die quickly in a cloud of stinging bees than to choke to death.

One or two bees still crawled weakly across the floor, but none came to sting her. The air was so thick with smoke she could hardly breathe, and as she stepped out of the fountain basin, her fur plastered to her body, some instinct made her lower her muzzle until her nose was close to the floor. Here the air was more breathable, but it still made her cough and gasp.

There was only one way to get to the jungle outside, and as she looked at the passage her eyes narrowed and she shrank back. Great red and orange flames were visible, leaping and writhing like living things. Sometimes she could see nothing but fire, then the flames would die for a second or so, and the land beyond would be visible. Out there was where she wanted to be, but before she could make up her mind to dash for freedom the flames would sweep across the exit again.

Whimpering at the heat, Dum-dum scrambled back into the water and submerged herself, but it was no escape. The air was growing ever more suffocatingly thick with smoke and fumes. She could either stay there and die miserably, or make a desperate dash for the open air.

Her heart was thumping with terror as she leaped out of the water. She did not want to face that barrier of flames, but when for an instant the flames seemed less, she sprang forward.

As if the fire had been tempting her, the flames roared across the escape route again even as she began to bound forward, but this time she did not draw back. Had the passage not been straight she might have died, for she ran with her eyes shut. She stumbled once as she put a paw on a loose stone, then she was in the heart of the flames.

For a split second her ears were filled with the crackle of burning brushwood, but the gauntlet of fire she had to pass through was no more than three yards long. Suddenly the terrifying noises were less, and the heat on her closed eyes had gone. In great bounds Dum-dum went on, and some seconds passed before she realized the danger was behind her.

She opened her eyes, and there was neither fire nor smoke ahead of her, only sun-parched grassland dotted with trees. Sobbing for breath, she stopped and then turned to look back.

Behind her the air was black with a rising column

of smoke, and at its foot flames were leaping. Sparks swept out as some bamboo joints exploded. Seen through it all, already soot-marked, were the outlines of the building. When the fire was gone, some passing peasant would gape in wonder at the sight of a ruined building he had never suspected was there.

Dum-dum was steaming as she stood there, unaware that she owed her safety to the fact that she had been well soaked in water before making her desperate dash for life. Her wet fur had saved her from serious injury. Her whiskers were singed, and were now mere stubs an inch long. Before the fire they had been five times that length.

After shaking the remaining water from her fur, Dum-dum lay down and began to lick her nose. It was swollen and very painful from the bee stings. There were also swellings on her back, but her fur had saved her from worse injury.

Behind her the fire continued to roar, but the sky was clearing as the sudden electrical storm that had started the blaze began drifting away. Over many hundreds of square miles anxious villagers had watched the storm. They had hoped it would mean the beginning of the overdue monsoon rains, but the clouds thinned out. The grumble of thunder died away, and the sun burst forth once more, blazing down with all its hot-season fury.

Some miles south of where Dum-dum lay, old Ram Chatterjee and his assistant saw the rising column of smoke, but they were not interested. Fires at the end of the dry season were common. Their interest lay in finding the missing cheetah.

With a skill that brought grudging admiration from Shar Lal, the older man had followed Dum-dum's footprints from the stable gates across the dusty plain. In the windless morning he read correctly the story of her chase of the big sambar stag.

He had even guessed the story of the red dogs, for one of them lay dead in the mud by the sluggishly flowing stream. Crossing by the stepping stones, he admitted his luck when he picked up the trail again, but when they came to the fringes of the jungle, Ram had to confess himself beaten. It was impossible to follow any animal over ground littered by dead leaves.

"No use going in there," he said. "We'll turn back to the plain. Dum-dum won't stay in the jungle. Cheetahs are not jungle hunters, and if she wants to eat she'll have to come out where she can run down a buck."

"She might not leave the jungle," Shar Lal pointed out. "What then?"

"She *will* leave it," Ram insisted. "A cheetah hunts by speed. She's got to race alongside a running animal and bring it down that way. Tigers and leopards can stalk a sambar stag or a chital hind, but cheetahs kill on the run. That's why I know our cheetah will return to the plain."

"If she doesn't, we'll both be out of work," Shar Lal commented.

"I tell you she'll come back to the plain," Ram snapped, "*and* we'll catch her." He spoke as if he were absolutely certain, but deep down he was not sure.

Dum-dum did return to the plain. She was desperately hungry, for the one bandicoot she had caught had scarcely been big enough to take the edge off her appetite.

Half an hour before sunset a strange thing happened. Some hundreds of yards away she saw a small herd of buck feeding. She did not get their scent because the wind was in the wrong direction, yet even as she noticed them they began to run. Stiffening, she watched. They were not running away, but toward her!

The low drumming of hooves grew louder. The herd was fanning out, but one animal was heading straight for her, his head held high. Dum-dum crouched down. This was something that had never happened before, and she waited tense and ready.

She brought the buck down so quickly he never

knew what killed him, and then, as Dum-dum stood with one forepaw on the dead animal's neck, she saw the reason for the panic-stricken flight of the herd. Eyes blazing, mouth wide in a threatening snarl, another cheetah appeared.

He slithered to a full stop at sight of Dum-dum, who snarled threateningly. The newcomer, a slightly larger animal, came forward in a menacing stiff-legged walk. Then, for no apparent reason, the fury went out of his eyes. He sat down and, instead of snarling, began to purr.

Dum-dum watched him suspiciously, but some of the tenseness went out of her muscles. This was the first time she had seen another cheetah since she was a cub. What was more, this was a male cheetah.

For several minutes the big male squatted nearby, purring. Then he rose, and a moment later the two animals were sniffing at one another, and Dum-dum lost her fear of him. He licked her neck and ears until she was purring with delight, and it was a full half hour before Dum-dum's hunger made her turn to the buck and begin feeding.

The male cheetah led her to a spring where cold water bubbled from out some rocks. There they drank and cleaned themselves before finding a spot where the bushes would shelter them from the morning dew.

Dum-dum was hungry when she awoke. Her companion had eaten a tremendous meal, sufficient to last him for a day or so, but Dum-dum had never been accustomed to huge meals. Back at the stables there had always been some food for her each morning.

After stretching and yawning she pawed the still drowsy male, then turned and trotted away to look for the remains of the buck. Her companion followed at a more leisurely pace, for he was not interested in food.

When she was about a hundred yards away from the scattered bushes where the buck had been killed, Dum-dum paused, her ears pricked. Something was happening near their kill.

While she was still forty yards away she realized that the rest of the buck was rapidly vanishing into the stomachs of a score of four-legged thieves. Waiting for them to finish were half a dozen scrawny-necked vultures perched on the nearest trees, clashing their beaks like butchers sharpening their knives.

The thieves were red dogs, the same pack that had so nearly got Dum-dum when she was stuck in the river mud. They showed no alarm at sight of the approaching cheetah, but went on eating as if they were specially invited guests. Everything was calm and orderly.

# Freedom for a Cheetah

There was none of the feverish haste that jackals show when they are at a kill. They snap viciously at one another and tear off great gobbets of meat, bolting it down as if there is not a moment to spare. The wild dogs were different. They were like a well-drilled army patrol. The leader and one or two older dogs had been the first to eat and were now lying nearby, dozing or scratching for fleas. Others were eating, and the youngest members of the pack were standing waiting. They looked as if they were afraid of nothing.

Dum-dum arrived in their midst like a thunderbolt. Those who were eating heard the first alarmed whimperings of the older dogs and started to leap away. The cheetah's flailing paws scattered them into a panic-stricken rush for safety. One dog died with a broken back, another was rolled over and then limped away with a broken hind leg.

The rest of the pack scattered, tails down, at the fury of the attack, but by the time they had raced fifty yards away their panic faded. The leader looked back, saw that the cheetah was not pursuing, and turned. Two minutes after Dum-dum burst on them, the wild dogs were squatting in a half circle around her, whimpering uneasily and looking at their leader.

Dum-dum glared at them examining the remains of the kill. There was precious little of the buck left, and what was left was not the best of the meat. She plucked at a piece and snarled as she got the scent of dog on it. A whining from twenty yards away made her look up. Her companion was standing there, trying to coax her into coming away and leaving the carcass for the dogs.

Dum-dum's fury of a minute or so earlier was now gone. She might have loped across to join her new mate if the circle of red dogs had not tightened, barring her way. A big red female had been sniffing at the dog Dum-dum had killed. He had been her mate, and when she left him to join the pack circle her eyes were glowing with a greenish fire.

Dum-dum took a pace forward toward her mate, and a moment later felt a sharp pain in her tail. Whirling around, she leaped at a dog that had darted in to fasten his teeth in her tail before leaping back to join the circle of dogs.

Uneasiness gripped Dum-dum and she started forward, meaning to join her newfound mate. She expected the dogs to move out of her way, but they stood their ground, silently snarling to show they did not fear her. Dum-dum could have overwhelmed two or three of them with little trouble, but there were twenty of them. She stopped, and looked over the heads of the dogs at the big male cheetah.

He whined pleadingly, asking her to come. He knew that their only chance of keeping a whole skin was to get away. In a stand-up fight even two cheetahs could not defeat a pack of these ferocious red dogs.

Dum-dum tried again to join him, but the dogs were too clever. Six of them turned and trotted toward the male cheetah. They were like policemen ordering someone to move on. Snarling, Dum-dum's mate turned and trotted slowly away.

Desperate at the thought of losing him, Dum-dum suddenly leaped over the pack, risking death by the rash act. Two dogs jumped at her, but their snapping jaws closed on thin air.

The big male cheetah stopped at the sudden commotion, but there were still six of the red dogs between him and Dum-dum. They hurled themselves at her as she came bounding up, and she was forced to turn aside.

From that moment she never had another chance to try and rejoin her mate. The red dogs ran on either side of her, whimpering, but making no attempt to bring her down.

Stretching her legs, she raced away at a speed not one of the dogs could hope to match, yet when she stopped to regain her breath, the pack was not so far behind. They ran at a tireless speed that enabled them to go on and on and on.

They surrounded her, and when their panting had died away they began the hit-and-run attacks. One dog would make a rush from behind, forcing Dum-dum to leap to her feet, but at the last moment the dog would swerve out of reach. At the same time another dog would rush in from the front. It was an age-old game to tire her out. There would come a time when she would be so exhausted that instead of swerving to one side a dog would close with her; then the rest of the pack would rush in to finish her off.

Twice she saw her mate. The big male cheetah had followed, but was keeping at a safe distance. He must have known it was too dangerous to try and interfere, yet he would not desert Dum-dum completely.

Dum-dum rose after about half an hour of meeting the hit-and-run attacks. Much of her panic had gone now. She leaped over the dogs facing her and headed across country, not at a mile-eating gallop, but at a comfortable swinging canter.

Dum-dum might have outrun their endurance, or they might have seen some other, easier prey and left her in peace, but the wild dogs were driven on by a strange urge to avenge a dead member of the pack. They would keep on Dum-dum's trail until she could not take another step. That would be the moment for the final reckoning.

## chapter six
## The Long Chase

Dum-dum ran for miles across a grassless plain where there was no shade of any kind and where the ground was so hot it scorched the pads of her feet. Her head was beginning to droop when she finally ran down a dried-up ravine and saw a place to rest: a hollow in the bank, scooped out by monsoon floods. In there Dum-dum could not be attacked from the rear. If the dogs tried to attack they would have to leap up several feet to get to her.

When the pack arrived a minute or so later the dogs flopped down in a half circle, tongues

96

hanging, flanks heaving. They made no attempt to get at her. But by midafternoon Dum-dum realized she had another enemy she could not beat—thirst!

The wild dogs, who must have known this part of the countryside well, went off in twos and threes, and it was obvious they had gone to drink. Somewhere nearby there was water. Dum-dum was wilting; she must have water. In India the heat in the summer gets halfway to boiling point, and there can come a time when, without water, man or beast will die.

Then, in the hot silence of midafternoon, Dum-dum suddenly heard the male cheetah's deep-throated purring. She looked up. The half circle of dogs arose, tense and expectant. There he was, across the ravine, a splendid pale-gold animal, spotted with black dots.

Dum-dum came back to life. Seconds earlier her eyes had been lackluster. Now they shone with new hope. She called back to him while the dogs, whining in sudden excitement, trotted this way and that as if wondering if the newcomer would leap down into the ravine and try to get to his mate.

For a minute or more the male cheetah stared across at Dum-dum. He whined continuously, trying to persuade her to join him. Then, as if he knew she was trapped, he bounded down into the ravine, and as the pack turned to rush at him, he raced away again. He was trying to draw off the dogs to give his newfound mate a chance at freedom.

The red dogs were too clever for that. A sudden whining from the pack leader made them hesitate. Then some returned to keep watch over Dum-dum while the rest pursued her mate.

Dum-dum watched and waited, her eyes glowing with excitement and hope. At the end of ten minutes the first of the dogs that had gone after the male cheetah trotted back, and soon the rest of them reappeared. It had been a brave rescue attempt, but there had been too many dogs and the male cheetah had been forced to run for his life.

The dogs began to settle down again, dozing off one by one, but a few always remained alert, pretending to search for fleas, yet never taking their eyes off the cheetah.

Dum-dum also settled down, but not to sleep. She waited for perhaps half an hour, and then, when the dogs seemed really settled, she bounded down into the ravine. Her first leap carried her easily over the heads of the nearest dogs.

In seconds the silence was gone. The pack arose and was in full pursuit at once. They whimpered excitedly, as if sure that they would soon finish the long chase.

Within a minute Dum-dum saw where the dogs had gone to drink, for near the end of the ravine was a small pool. Several deer were drinking there, and they fled at the sight of her.

Dum-dum was desperate for water, but the pack was some fifty yards behind her, and would have been at her throat had she stopped. Ahead of her was a high bank. Through a tiny gap near the bottom came the water for the pool.

Dum-dum hurled herself up the bank, and for a moment what she saw made her pause at the top. There was the same man-made river where she had been trapped in the mud. The scene was unchanged. A narrow ribbon of water ran down the center, with a stretch of treacherously soft mud on each side of it. Even when Dum-dum had been chasing the sambar stag, and had been fresh and strong, she had not been able to leap far enough to avoid the muddy death trap. Now she was far too tired even to consider trying to leap across.

Turning left, she loped along the bank top, hoping to see some place where she would be able to cross. She came to the narrow bridge used by natives when monsoon floods filled the river from bank to bank. Less than fifty yards beyond were the stepping stones. They were the same ones she had used when she had been floating down the stream.

Freedom for a Cheetah

Disregarding the steps the villagers had cut in the bank to help them climb up and down, Dum-dum dropped to river level in a single graceful bound. She reached the stepping stones and, without a pause, leaped from stone to stone.

The leader of the red dogs followed almost at her heels. He was panting in his eagerness, for he could tell that the cheetah was tired, very tired. If he could get a grip on her tail just before she got across the stepping stones, the battle was won. The rest of the dogs were crowding behind him, and they could swarm all over the cheetah before she had a chance to make him loosen his grip.

He pressed forward, but before he could snatch at the tail that swayed only a foot in front of him, Dum-dum stopped and turned around. Whatever the risk, she must have water! Swinging a paw at the pack leader, she only just missed knocking him into the sluggishly flowing stream. As he inched as far back on his stone as he could, she dipped her muzzle and lapped up a little water.

Lifting her head hurriedly as the pack leader inched nearer, she snarled and forced him to back away again. Down went her head once more and her tongue lapped furiously. She needed a long, deep drink, yet even the little she had managed to get put new life and hope into her.

The rest of the pack was pressing onto the stepping stones and whining with eagerness. They were urging their leader to force the cheetah on and over to the other side. If she slaked her thirst she would find new strength for another long run, and in an hour the sun would be setting. They were all anxious for a meal. The younger dogs were so impatient they were crowding two to a stone and were in danger of forcing some members of the pack into the stream or, what was worse, into the deadly mud.

Suddenly sensing that she could not be attacked either from the side or the rear, Dum-dum began to drink more leisurely. She had to keep a watchful eye on the pack leader, however, for each time she lowered her muzzle to the water he would inch forward threateningly. Time after time she was forced to swing her head up and threaten him with her right paw.

Suddenly a dog just behind the leader grew so impatient that he tried a foolish trick in the hope of forcing Dum-dum to retreat. He leaped onto the stone already occupied by the pack leader. For a moment it seemed as if the move would succeed, for the cheetah retreated to the next stepping stone.

The two dogs advanced, leaping across onto the stone Dum-dum had just left, but it was a mistake for which they paid dearly. The rest of the wild dogs were so keen to finish the hunt that they, too, moved forward one stone, and when Dum-dum turned and sprang back onto the stone she had just left, neither the pack leader nor the dog with him had room to move. When they tried to get out of her way they slipped off the stone and into the water.

To add to the confusion, the two dogs on the next stone also panicked. Seeing the cheetah standing on the stepping stone where their leader and his second-in-command had been but a moment before, they tried to turn back.

As a team the wild dogs were almost unbeatable, and more than a match for any cheetah, but spread out on the stepping stones, they were not a team. The two dogs now in the path of the spitting, snarling Dum-dum refused to face her. One tried to retreat, and the other was swept into the water by a flailing blow from a powerful right paw. The other dog half turned, made a wild leap, and went straight into the treacherous mud at the water's edge.

The pack was completely disorganized now. Three of them were floundering in the shallow water and a fourth was stuck fast in the mud. The pack began to withdraw, whining in their anxiety.

One of the three dogs in the water tried to get

out over the thin crust of mud and was lucky enough to struggle back to the water when it broke under his weight. The other two were already thirty yards downstream, paddling along and not knowing quite what to do.

Dum-dum was glad enough to flop down onto her stone, for now the rest of the pack had retreated to the bank. With no leader to guide them they padded uneasily to and fro, whining anxiously. Had they been able to close in on her from all sides the fight would have been short, but where they had to face her singly she had all the advantages, and the pack did not know how to tackle the problem.

To add to Dum-dum's temporary relief, her new mate appeared on the riverbank some sixty yards away. He could not come nearer, because the dogs were too many for him, but his presence gave Dum-dum new confidence. Something was bound to happen soon, and when it did he would be there to help her.

Twice in the next half hour half a dozen of the wild dogs chased the male cheetah away, but each time he returned, silent and watchful. By now, however, some of Dum-dum's confidence began to fade. She had hoped the wild dogs would tire and perhaps begin to drift off, but they gave no sign of doing anything like that. Some lay down, others padded restlessly to and fro; all kept their gaze on the cheetah.

It was an armed truce that could not last. Dum-dum dared not leave her vantage point. The moment she crossed the river the pack would be at her heels. Yet if she stayed here the end was inevitable. The dogs could beat her in a long siege. There was food along the river: rats, mice, and other tidbits to keep the dogs from getting hungry, but Dum-dum could get nothing.

Dum-dum whined anxiously to her mate, but the male cheetah was powerless to help. If he tried to get to her the dogs would pull him down in minutes.

Then, after a time, and for no apparent reason, the pack's uneasy whining and trotting about ceased. The dogs stood and stared past Dum-dum. For a moment or so she did not know what was happening. Only when one of the dogs started to come across the stepping stones again did she swivel and look toward the opposite bank. To her amazement and alarm, two more wild dogs were there. They were panting after a hard run, and their coats were so muddy they looked more gray-brown than red. They were two of the three dogs that had been knocked into the water earlier. They had managed to get ashore when they reached a small tree that had been washed down during the last monsoon floods.

Dum-dum's eyes were green with hate and fear as she looked at the two dogs on the bank. Behind her was the rest of the pack, and already several of them were coming out onto the stepping stones. If she stayed where she was the two dogs would come down off the bank onto the stepping stones, and she would be caught with no hope of escape.

She turned away from the dogs now streaming out onto the stones. Two magnificent bounds took her across the remaining stepping stones and onto the hard-baked earth. Now, if she wanted to reach the open plain beyond, she had to pass the two dogs on top of the bank.

There was no time to pause and think. Behind her, a whining, excited pack was following her across the stepping stones. Above her, and with every advantage of position, were the pack leader and another of the older dogs. They had an almost unbeatable position. They had only to lunge at her as she came up the bank, and she would be sent rolling down to the pack below.

Dum-dum turned and ran along the foot of the bank. The two dogs on top also ran, while behind her came the rest of the pack. Ahead, the ribbon of water wriggled this way and that like a snake until, after running some eighty yards, Dum-dum saw that the stream of water, and with it the soft mud, swerved toward the ground on which she was running.

There was nothing to do now but to face the bank or the pack at her heels. Swerving, she made a mighty diagonal leap upward, hoping to get to the top of the bank before the leader of the pack and his second-in-command got there. It was not one of her best leaps. She was almost two feet from the top when her forepaws scraped frantically at the hard earth and failed to get a grip!

# chapter seven
# Death or—?

For a moment the cheetah seemed to hang there, her four paws close together. Her eyes were blazing, her jaws were wide in a menacing snarl. Above her the leader of the red dogs and his comrade were waiting, tongues lolling, triumph in their eyes. Below Dum-dum the pack came racing up, and one bolder than the rest made a quick leap and snapped at the end of the cheetah's waving tail.

It was a brave effort to drag her down, and it could have succeeded had the cheetah not suddenly turned. She was beginning to slide down the bank anyway, but gathering her powerful hind legs under her, she gave a tremendous leap down the bank and back the way she had come.

She landed, paws wide, on three dogs, and one was quick enough to turn his jaws upward and take a hurried bite at her creamy-colored under-parts. He slashed the skin, and got a mouthful of hairs, bringing a half-strangled yelp of pain from Dum-dum.

She bounded on, then turned again to the bank. This time she got out on top before the leader of the pack was within ten feet of her. In a moment the rest of the dogs were scrambling after her, and once they were on top, they took up the chase. It seemed as if the leader had passed a message to the pack: they had spent too much time trailing this cheetah. She was tiring now, and they should close in quickly and make their kill.

At the end of a quarter of a mile Dum-dum had gained a lead of a hundred yards, but she was sobbing for breath. She was built for short bursts of terrific speed while her pursuers were accustomed to running for hour after hour, patiently wearing down their intended victim.

Dum-dum dared not take the rest she needed. She had to go on, galloping for a hundred yards, then trotting a little. The red dogs kept at the same speed, and with no sign of weakening they steadily began to cut down the cheetah's lead.

At the end of three miles Dum-dum stopped and turned. She had come to the point where she thought she would face the pack. But the chorus of eager whines and the red, lolling tongues of the dogs made her change her mind. She might kill and maim a few of them, but if she stood and fought she would certainly die.

She turned and bounded off again, but this time her burst of speed was very short. Her slim legs felt like lead and deep though her chest was, she could not get enough air.

Running more slowly now, she headed east. The pack was within fifty yards of her when she saw something ahead of her that gave her new hope. Moving north, and no more than three hundred yards away, was a bullock cart, its ungreased axles filling the air with a horrible screeching and whining. There were two men with it.

From somewhere Dum-dum found a little extra strength. A spurt of speed drew her away from the red dogs for a moment or so. Then her pace slackened again, and the pack began to close in once more.

The chase had not gone unnoticed. Once they were sure what kind of animals were coming their way, the men tried to hurry on their plodding bullocks. They whacked the poor beasts over their bony hindquarters and at the same time bellowed curses at the approaching cheetah and the pursuing wild dogs. The men grabbed the wire-bound cudgels they always carried in the cart. If they lost their bullocks their livelihood was gone. They would rather face a tiger than see the two bullocks dead.

Dum-dum heard the uproar, but she was accustomed to human voices and did not swerve an inch from her course. The men reminded her of Ram Chatterjee, who had taken her out so often in the cool of the morning to chase the fleet-footed black buck. That the voices of the men were not familiar did not put her off. In this moment of danger she was coming back to the things she knew, and she knew men.

Straight for the cart she came, covering the dusty ground in great bounds. The younger of the two men moved to meet her, swinging his wire-bound cudgel. If he had stood his ground he might have easily felled the cheetah, but at the very last moment his courage deserted him and he flung himself to one side.

In the desperate need of the moment Dum-dum scarcely saw him. Her eyes were on the jolting, creaking cart. If she could get onto that, the wild dogs would have to jump up to attack her, and she would have an advantage.

The cart swayed wildly as she leaped onto it, but

she had long ago learned how to balance on a moving cart. Regaining her balance in a flash, she turned to face the dogs. The pack was in full cry, and not twenty yards away.

Showing amazing courage, the two men stood their ground, yelling and waving their cudgels, determined to defend their bullocks. The wild dogs swerved, half going to the left, the other half to the right; then they closed in on the bullock cart. Without hesitation the leader leaped in to attack.

In the minutes that followed there was a battle that was to be talked of in the villages for many months to come. Strangely enough, the two bullocks played a big part in it. Seeing the dogs, they suddenly took fright and broke into an awkward gallop.

The creaking cart gave a faster jerk forward just as the leader of the pack alighted near Dum-dum. His slashing teeth missed their aim only because of the sudden increased speed of the cart. A moment later Dum-dum gave him a buffet across the side of the head which sent him cartwheeling backwards. As he fell he knocked over two more dogs in midleap.

Dum-dum had two splendid allies in the men. Both graybeard and the younger man were so terrified that their bullocks might be killed that they forgot their fears for themselves. Yelling like

madmen, they leaped at the dogs with their wire-bound cudgels. They knocked over dog after dog; the cudgels were deadly weapons.

Dum-dum, too, was putting up the fight of her life. Balanced on the moving cart, she beat off attack after attack with paws and teeth. The air was filled with the terrified bawling of the bullocks, the yells of the men, and the whining of the excited dogs. It was too fierce to last.

The fight ended as suddenly as it had begun. The frightened bullocks, exhausted by their stampede, slowed down and then stopped. They could not have galloped another yard, even if a thousand dogs had come.

The two men suddenly realized that the attackers had drawn off. As the dust began to settle, they could see the remains of the pack, three bruised dogs, standing a dozen yards away. The others, dead or dying, were scattered over the plain. Some were trying groggily to get to their feet. They were the ones that had been knocked out by a cudgel blow on the head.

On the bullock cart itself there was an untidy heap of bodies: several dead or dying red dogs and, under them, the pale-gold body of the cheetah.

The two men were dripping with sweat, and the younger one was bleeding from a dog bite in his right arm. The wound was painful, but for the moment he was too flushed with triumph to feel it.

Picking up a stone the young man flung it at the watching dogs. One gave a startled yell and raced away; the other two followed. Then to the amazement of the men a spotted golden form rose from the dust, stared at them, then followed the wild dogs at a much slower pace.

"Did you see that, Chandra? There was a second cheetah out there. Oh, if we had only had a rifle."

"That would be this cheetah's mate," the older man said, and wiping the sweat from the end of his nose, he added, "But what a tale to tell in the village, eh? What a fight! And when we show them what we have on the cart no one can doubt our story."

"And there is the cheetah's skin," the young man said eagerly. "The skins of red dogs are worth something, but a cheetah's skin—that will be worth more than a handful of rupees."

The older man shook his head doubtfully.

"I would not start thinking of the rupees we will get for this cheetah's skin," he suggested. "If her hide is not torn to shreds I shall be greatly surprised. The dogs must have bitten her in a thousand places. Anway, when we have skinned her we shall see."

Three evenings later Ram Chatterjee walked wearily into his little house and dropped his empty food bag on the floor. Then he put his old rifle and his bag of cartridges in their usual place.

"Don't ask me if I have got her," he said sadly as his wife came in from the other room. "Just get me some food, for I starve."

To his surprise his wife laughed. It was not the scornful laugh he had expected—for she had insisted he would never find the missing cheetah. Her laugh was a happy one. Laying a hand gently on her husband's shoulder, she said, "Wash, husband, and lift thy head again, for I have good news."

"She has come back?" That was the only good news Ram could think of. But his eyes clouded again when his wife shook her head.

"She has not come back—yet."

Ram's eyes glowed afresh. Now he knew the cheetah must be somewhere near. His wife told him about a visit two days earlier of a man from a nearby village. He was a young man, and one arm was heavily bandaged. He had come with a tale of a terrible fight between wild dogs and a cheetah.

"He came here because the story had been told in the bazaar of how our cheetah had escaped, and how your master had given you a week to find her."

"So even in the villages they know," Ram murmured sadly. "And soon they will all know I did not find her myself."

"Not so," his wife said. "This man came to me secretly. He thought that you might reward him if he let *you* take the cheetah back. He knows that if you take her back it will bring you honor. Everyone knows you are a good man, and he wanted to help you. I said you would reward him for his kindness."

For a few moments Ram Chatterjee was too overcome with joy to be able to speak. If he had been dismissed it would have been a disgrace hard to bear. If he could tell his master that the cheetah was back in her stable, that would be a moment he would never forget.

"Aie—aie, wife, I am a lucky man, a very lucky man."

"Wash while I prepare food," his wife urged. "Then go to the village and see this man. He said that the cheetah had many wounds, but he did not think she would die."

"If she is alive I can make her well again," Ram said quietly. "And I am sure of this: once she is back with me she will never want to escape again. She is not fitted for the life of a wild cheetah. She does not know how to care for herself. This freedom will have taught her a lesson she will never forget."

Four days passed before Dum-dum was strong

enough to be brought back to her stable. In the weeks that followed Ram spent many hours attending to her wounds and massaging her stiff muscles. Often, after the sun had set, he would go and sit with her in the darkened stable. He did not speak, did not even touch her; he just sat and watched. Time after time she would go to the iron-barred window. Thrusting her nose as far as she could through the bars, she would sniff deeply of the scents carried on the night breeze.

One night Ram confessed to his wife, "If I were a rich man I would take my cheetah out to the very center of the plain and set her free. She is unhappy. She is full grown now, and should have a mate and kittens of her own."

For a moment his wife stared at him, fear and anger in her expression. Then she said sharply, "Don't talk like a fool. If you set her free you would not only lose your job, but would go to prison. The cheetah belongs to your master. If you set her free, who will feed me while you are in prison? If you set that animal free, you lose your job at least, and we also lose our house."

"I know," Ram agreed soberly. "I love her as I would love a son, but I know I cannot free her. I was only saying what I would like to do—if I were a rich man."

"You are not a rich man," his wife insisted, "and if you lose this job we shall starve."

Ram Chatterjee sighed and turned away. For almost a week he went about with a sad look in his eyes, yet strangely enough when he was told to prepare the cheetah for a hunt because guests were coming for the weekend, he suddenly became brighter.

On the morning of the hunt he rose early and went out to prepare Dum-dum for the hunt. He was surprised when he entered the stable to discover his wife there. She pointed an accusing finger at the large bowl of meat scraps he carried and said bitterly, "I have often wakened in the night and groaned to hear you talking in your sleep. Now you have talked in your sleep once too often."

"What do you mean?" Ram Chatterjee laid the bowl of meat against the stable wall, as far from the sniffing, hungry Dum-dum as possible.

"I woke two nights ago and you were laughing to yourself," his wife said. "Then you spoke of making sure the cheetah went free. You would give her a good feed on the morning of the hunt. You knew she was longing for her freedom, and if she was well fed, she would chase away after the buck, but would not make a kill. Instead, she would run away and be gone forever. Free . . . free—that was what you were saying. Husband, you are a fool."

In the yellow light of the stable lamp Ram Chatterjee slowly nodded his head. "You are right, wife. That is what I did plan. I *am* a fool. Take the meat away. Dum-dum shall not go free."

His wife stayed in the stable until Shar Lal arrived and the oxcart came rumbling into the stable yard. Dum-dum was loaded on, and they went off into the cool of early dawn.

Half an hour after they had reached the appointed place the car bringing Dum-dum's owner and his guests arrived. Armed with powerful binoculars, they were looking forward keenly to seeing the cheetah in action, and came over to admire Dum-dum as she stood on the cart, the soft leather hood still masking her eyes.

When all was ready the bullock cart creaked slowly across the plain in the direction of the nearest herd of antelope, while the Rolls-Royce followed with Dum-dum's owner and his guests.

The servants and helpers from a nearby village all waited expectantly, for they knew there would be gifts for them if the chase was successful. Two hundred yards away a man rose and waved his arms. They were near enough to the antelope for Dum-dum to be released.

The cart was stopped, and Ram Chatterjee went forward, leading the cheetah by a loosely looped thong about her neck. It would be slipped in a second when the moment was right.

Dum-dum was trembling a little and sniffing the air. She had got the first faint scent of the antelope. She was always like this before a hunt, for she was hungry. The secret of Ram Chatterjee's success as a cheetah trainer was in keeping Dum-dum short of food for a day or so before the hunt. The hungrier she was, the faster she ran, knowing she would be well fed at the end of the chase.

The man who had signaled that there were antelope ahead came back to point through the thinning morning mist. "See the big buck, Ram Chatterjee? I have never seen so magnificent a buck in my life. Do you see him?"

Ram nodded and, dropping to one knee, he turned Dum-dum's head until she was looking in the right direction. For some seconds she showed no interest. Then Ram felt the muscles of her shoulders tighten. Not only had she got the scent, but she had caught sight of the big buck.

"She is ready, master. May I loose her?" Ram called, and got a nod from Dum-dum's owner when he was sure that his guests were in a position to get the best possible view of the hunt. A moment later the soft leather thong was slipped from about the cheetah's neck. Ram Chatterjee patted her, and with a low whimper of excitement Dum-dum moved away from the group. The hunt was on.

For the next three or four minutes no one spoke. The two men who were watching this kind of hunt for the first time found it more thrilling than they had thought possible. For Dum-dum's owner, who had seen his cheetah hunt many times, it was to be a morning he would never forget.

Dum-dum went toward the antelope at a fair speed, but keeping as close to the ground as possible. She was still three hundred yards from the antelope when the big black buck raised his head and stared suspiciously toward her. Dum-dum crouched down, remaining so motionless that she seemed to become part of the ground itself. Even the watchers using binoculars suddenly found themselves having difficulty picking her out.

The buck lowered his head. Dum-dum bounded forward once more, but the buck had been alarmed and looked up again almost immediately. Dum-dum froze, but she had been seen. The buck gave a mighty leap into the air, the better to see what this danger was. Dum-dum threw caution to the winds then and began to race toward him in a series of tremendous bounds that ate up the distance.

"Ride!" Ram Chatterjee yelled, and dug his heels into the bony ribs of his horse. Shar Lal was left yards behind, his tin of raw meat swinging wildly from his saddle. The watchers in the Rolls-Royce kept their binoculars on the cheetah and marveled at the exhibition of speed they were seeing.

The herd scattered, the hinds racing away in a series of fantastic leaps. But their lord and master wasted no strength in high leaping; he was running like the wind, and Dum-dum was after him.

Fast though the buck ran, the cheetah was faster. This was her first outing since being mauled by the red dogs, and she seemed to have a new zest for the hunt, which added to her speed. By the time the buck had covered a hundred yards, Dum-dum had covered a hundred and fifty. At the end of a quarter of a mile the cheetah was almost alongside the black buck.

"She'll have him now," one of the excited guests yelled. "Oh, what speed! She must be the fastest hunter in the world. She's like a yellow bullet."

No one else spoke. The morning mists had been sucked up by the sun now and the air was clear enough for them all to see the end of the chase. They saw the buck swerve, his hooves kicking up extra large puffs of yellow dust. Then came a small explosion of dust.

"He's down—he's down!" There was a chorus of cries, and Dum-dum's owner nodded his satisfaction. This had been one of the better chases. Now it was left for Ram Chatterjee and his assistant to grab the cheetah before she could start eating the kill. The two men were racing up as fast as their lean horses could take them.

Out there, with the yellow dust beginning to settle around her, Dum-dum's eyes were blazing with the excitement of the chase. Suddenly she lifted her head and sniffed. The light morning wind was bringing a scent to her, the scent of another cheetah: her mate.

As Ram Chatterjee and Shar Lal galloped nearer, Dum-dum suddenly bounded away from the dead black buck. Eyes glowing with joy, she raced across the plain to where the male cheetah was moving in her direction.

They stopped some yards apart. The big male gave a throaty little purr. Dum-dum drew her lips in the beginning of a soundless snarl, but it vanished as quickly as it started. Seconds later the cheetahs were rubbing cheeks and purring loudly.

Behind them came the drumming of hooves and the banging of a tin—the usual signal to Dum-dum that there was meat for her. Ram Chatterjee was desperately anxious now to let his master see that he was trying hard to recapture the cheetah.

# Death, or—?

The two cheetahs ceased their purring; both looked around. The riders were fifty yards away, but that was as near as they got. In mighty, effortless bounds, Dum-dum and her mate headed west, faster than any horse could gallop.

Ram Chatterjee and his assistant returned to the buck. One of the guests would get a pair of horns as a trophy, even if he and Shar Lal did lose their jobs because of what had happened. Yet there were no harsh words. The two guests had been so thrilled with the short chase and the lightning-quick kill that Dum-dum's late owner smiled with pride when the long spiral horns were held up for inspection.

Ram Chatterjee began to apologize for losing Dum-dum and was silenced with a wave of the hand. "There is no blame on you. We shall get another cheetah as soon as possible. It was a good hunt, and when you loose a cheetah there is always the risk that it will not stay to be captured again."

Ram Chatterjee gave a little bow of respect and thankfulness. He had lost the cheetah, but not his job. He could scarcely believe his good fortune.

When the hunting party got back to the big house and Ram broke the news of Dum-dum's escape to his wife she gave a long wail of horror. Then she yelled angrily, "It was your fault. You planned it. You wanted to set her free. Now—"

"Quiet, wife, quiet," Ram ordered. "I did want to set her free, but it was another man who took her away."

"Another man!" his wife gasped. "Who would dare do that?"

"A male cheetah." Her husband chuckled, and there was a twinkle in his eyes when he added, "And be glad I am not a cheetah, for Dum-dum's husband won't let his wife howl and shriek at him. He would cuff her across the head if she did. Now get me some food, for I am hungry."

"But your job?" his wife whimpered.

"It has been a good day for me," Ram Chatterjee said. "My cheetah is free, and I still have my job. Now—food, quickly."

Miles away, far from the big house and the villages, Dum-dum and her mate fed just before sundown on a barking deer. They went to a waterhole afterward to drink their fill and clean themselves. As the sun went down they found a comfortable spot and, with the hum of insects fading as the air grew cooler, settled down for the night. Dum-dum felt a peace and contentment she had never known before. She was free.

## ABOUT THE AUTHOR

Arthur Catherall is a well-known author of adventure stories for children. He enjoys exploring for himself the lands and regions in which he sets his tales. In addition to travels in India, Burma, and Ceylon he has climbed mountains in Lapland and Algeria, ridden camels in the Sahara, and sailed aboard trawlers and tramp steamers in the Arctic and the Atlantic.

Mr. Catherall's home is in Bolton, Lancashire, England.